For that special someone

CHAPTER ONE

To dream is a beautiful thing. You enter a world created by your imagination alone. Dreaming is loved, but equally feared by all of us. One such individual that dreaming touched in a strange way was a child called Alana. Alana could not wait to go to bed at night, contrary to most children her age. Alana was a happy child who enjoyed playing with her friends. She was a dreamer whose imagination often got the better of her. She often spent her waking hours daydreaming and anticipating her bedtime, often sleeping in the early evening hours and not waking up until her parents gently awoke her. It was known for Alana to sleep for more than 12 hours. Alana's dreams filled with full of fascination, adventure and fun. In her dreams, Alana did not have to pretend to be a princess or a ballet dancer, as she did in the playground with her friends. For in her dreams she truly could be what she wanted.

Our story begins on one particular night when Alana went to be tucked in by her mother at 7 pm sharp as per her usual routine. Alana was nine years old at the time and had possessed her dreaming phenomenon for all her life so far. She could remember every single dream she had ever had and even remembered everyone she had ever met in her dreams. Though dreams are believed to be merely a figment of our imaginations, Alana's dreaming phenomenon was much more than that. You might even say it could just be a reality. As Alana's eyes slowly closed, she felt herself drift off into her wonderful world of sleep. The familiar, relaxing feeling washed over her, and she forgot about the stresses and strains of being a 9-year old girl, which mostly consisted of wanting to grow up faster. While the boys who made her feel disgusted suddenly made her feel different.

Alana felt the natural, comfortable mattress beneath her body and the steady stream of golden sunlight settle on her eyelids. It was always daytime in this world. Alana steadily opened her eyes to see the golden sunlight bouncing off the white marble walls of the bedroom she was in. She smiled and looked around at her fairy tale. There was the window next to the bed framed in pure gold. Outside she could see lush green grass in the meadow with those odd, but beautiful trees with pale purple leaves dotted around. She turned her head to the right and could see her white stone dressing table with real makeup, not the fake cheap makeup you got at Christmas. Alana stretched her arms wide and leapt out of her luxurious double bed with golden sheets and simple white pillows then ran across the white marble floor towards the arched golden doorway. She flung the door open in eager anticipation, ran across the hallway, and let out a high-pitched whistle as her feet softly padded on the pristine floor. As she reached the huge winding staircase, she saw a black shadow rush across the hallway downstairs. Alana laughed and hurried down the stairs.

As she made her way down the staircase, she ran to the huge double back door, which was already partially open and hurried down the mosaic pattern patio steps onto the meadow. She felt the soft grass between her toes and smiled as the sun warmed her skin and made her white blonde hair sparkle as though she was a fairy. Suddenly she felt something hurl into her side and knock the air clean out of her lungs. She felt an enormous wet tongue on her face and opened her eyes to see her black German Shepherd, Zero, on her stomach wagging his tail vigorously.

"Zero!" Alana laughed and kissed her puppy's face.

"You're always so full of energy" Let's go and see our other friends shall we?

" Zero barked happily and took his paws off Alana with one last lick as Alana stood up and they ran together further into the meadow. Eventually, they stopped in front of a wooden gate with a post and rail fence. Alana climbed the gate to get a better look, as she was short for her age, while Zero put his paws on the bottom gate rung to look through the gap. Alana made a clicking sound with her tongue. For a moment it was silent, and all that could then be heard was Zero's quick panting and birds tweeting happily in the trees when suddenly, a familiar high-pitched whinny rang over the meadow and from between two trees emerged a bright white flash of mane and tail closely followed by a black flash. Galloping towards her were her two beloved horses Thunder, which was the black mare and Flash, which was the white horse. Alana quickly jumped over the gate, while Zero followed her by jumping through the gap in the gate rungs. They stood next to the gate as the two horses ran towards them, whinnying and tossing their heads all the time in delight. The two horses halted before Alana as she stroked them and spoke sweet nothings to them.

As Alana opened the gate, she looked at the two head collars draped over the fence and chuckled to herself. Alana got these two head collars when she got her two foals thinking she would need them, but never did, those horses trusted her with their life. As the four of them started to move towards the stables, Alana looked up at the castle in which she lived in her dream world. It was the most beautiful piece of architecture anyone had ever witnessed. The outside of the castle, made of pure silver, strengthened by white marble making it seem like silver rivers ran down the sides of the building with turrets of pure white being clouds. As they reached the stables, the two horses trotted into their two out of the ten private stables and stood in the entrance, quietly snickering to Alana. Alana chuckled,

"So, I suppose you both want your dinner, is that right?

"Zero, upon hearing the word dinner, put his front paws on Alana's leg and wagged his tail vigorously. Alana laughed and headed towards the feed shed, with Zero fast in tow.

They walked into the feed shed together, and Alana reached towards the big green feed bins at the back of the room. She looked around at the feed shed and on the wall were Flash and Thunder's saddles. She remembered the months it took her to break both the horses by herself. Even though they took it in their stride, not everything in her dream world could happen in an instant. In fact, not everything was under her control. It is true she could have anything she imagined, and sometimes it would just appear in front of her, but sometimes things had to be made from scratch, and even some things were impossible. Alana smiled at these memories as she prepared the feed for the horses and for Zero. She walked outside the stables with Zero and lay down his food bowl, then gave Thunder and Flash their food. Alana learnt on Thunder watching her eat while wondering what they were going to do. She glanced in the feed shed, saw the saddles, and bridles stacked on the wall and smiled; maybe today she would go on an extra long ride.

She stood there while everyone finished their food, then walked into the feed shed and first of all took Thunder's saddle off the saddle rack, then reached for her bridle which hung nearby. It was a lot for her to carry, but she managed to move it to Thunder's stable door and threw it over, so the saddle straddled the door and then threw the bridle over the top. Flash whinnied and started to nibble the saddle.

"I'm sorry, flash. You can still come.

"It'll be your turn to ride tomorrow," laughed Alana. She opened Thunder's stable and walked in, lugging the saddle off the door and placing it on Thunder's back. Alana then reached under her belly for the girth and buckled it up just right. She turned around to reach for her bridle and felt Thunder pulling at her top. Alana giggled and turned around to pet her on her nose. She bridled her up and lead her out to just outside the ménage where there was a mounting block, tying her up next to it. She walked back towards Flash's stable, opened the door, and walked out next to her. Alana whistled for Zero who, after finishing his dinner, had run off over the field to sniff around. Zero barrelled over to Alana while she mounted Thunder. She took the reins in her hands and clicked with her mouth at Thunder while giving him a little nudge. Thunder leapt forward into a trot, with Flash excited alongside and galloping straight off like a white rocket. Zero ran along barking in delight as Alana urged Thunder to pick up the pace.

The four of them galloped around the perimeter of Alana's house and out towards the front, where they went parallel to the road before swinging off into the forest nearby. Alana laughed in sheer bliss while she cantered head to head with Thunder and Zero. She looked up and saw the sunlight glistening through the leaves in the trees, making the floor of the forest look dappled. They took along the natural pathways in the woods, the horses kicking up mud with their hooves.

As they continued through the forest, they came out into a small clearing, which smelt of bluebells growing among the overgrown grass. As Alana rode through the wild grass, she started to pull on Thunder's reins slowing him down to stop, then climbed down holding onto his reins.

Alana then said to Thunder,

"Just wait a minute" as Thunder was eager to be passed, as he knew where they were heading.

Alana then walked over to a wooden gate, which was slightly overgrown with blackberry brambles and as Alana went to open the gate, there was two beautiful black and white magpies sat on the side eating blackberries. Alana then said

"Good morning magpies". They then nodded as if to say 'hello' back to Alana as they carried on eating the blackberries, then Alana carried on walking through the gate which led into the rich, lush meadows. Within a second, Thunder and Zero had gone running through the gate nearly knocking Alana of her feet. Alana then said to Thunder and Zero

"Watch where you're going!" with a little giggle, as they both ran past her to play on the Meadows.

As Alana put her feet on the bottom of the gate pushing the gate forward, the gate snapped shut. While Alana rested her feet on the edge of the gate, she looked up at the blackberries hanging down off the brambles, and then thought to herself

"These blackberries look sweet and juicy." As Alana leant forward, she began to pick the fruits with her tiny hands. And as she stood still on the bottom of the gate eating the blackberries as she picked them of the brambles, Alana stood watching Thunder, Flash and Zero playing in the sunlight, then climbs down from the gate and says to herself

"It's a lovely summer's day." Alana then decides to go off skipping to pick some daisies and notices a bunch of dandelions, so she changes her mind and goes off to collect a bunch of dandelions, which she then started to blow. Shortly after blowing the dandelions, she sees some lovely pale pink lilies growing on the edge of a wooden bridge and picks a bunch of them.

CHAPTER TWO

As Alana slowly started to walk on the wooden bridge, she stood still for a few seconds to admire the lovely surroundings. The sweet smell of the pink and red orchids was overpowering and made Alana feel drowsy as she felt her eyes starting to close. The next thing she knew, she woke up under a red willow tree still holding the bunch of daisies in one hand and a bunch of pale pink lilies in the other.

Alana then looks around and notices that everything is all red. As she sat on the red grass, she began to feel lost; she then wondered to herself 'How am I going to get home'. As she realises she has lost Thunder and Zero, her eyes started to fill up with tears. Within a few minutes, her tears began to stream down her cheeks as she cries to herself 'I am lost', 'I just want to go home', as she became more upset with herself.

Shortly after she heard the sweetest little voice comes from behind her;

"Whatever is the matter, my sweet little princess? "' Alana then looks around and notices there is a little green tinted skinned elf stood behind her. As it happens, the elf had been picking berries. The elf had the most beautiful red rose plaits growing in her hair. Alana then tells the little Elf that she is lost. She then goes on to inform the elf that she was in her very own perfect place, then had seen a wooden bridge, so she took a few steps and then woke up to find herself sat here.

"Please" said the elf "Come with me, I will help you",' as the friendly little elf leant forward stretching out her little green hand to help Alana up from where she sat. Alana then wipes away her tears with the back of her hand. A smile started to appear, and then with a little giggle, Alana took hold of the elf's hand once back up on her feet.

The friendly elf then leads the way across the beautiful red grass. After a few minutes, they came to an admirable flowing red river with the red-hot sun beaming down on them in the beautiful red forest.

As Alana and the friendly little elf entered the beautiful red forest, the elf says to Alana

"Not much further to go now". They then took a few short steps and a sharp left.

"Here we are, Welcome to the Strawberry Lagoon," said the little elf.

"It is so classy," said Alana as she glanced around with her eyes gleaming with excitement.

The elf then picks up a dandelion fairy from the pile of fairies, holds it in the palm of her hand, and says to Alana.

"You wished for an adventure." Within a quick flash, the dandelion fairy disappears, and Alana's two horses Thunder, Flash and the dog Zero all appear with the light. Alana and the elf both jump on to horses and start galloping with Zero running alongside them through the red forest, as they head towards the clear golden river.

As Alana and the little elf reached the beautiful pure golden river, they climbed off their horses. They then saw a small stone bridge, which they began to cross, holding on to the horse's reins as the two horses paddled through the water beside the stone bridge. The bridge was too rough for Thunder and Flash to walk across and for zero he seemed to be enjoying himself, running back and forth in the river splashing the water with his front paws.

Once across the golden river and through the dense forest, they came out into a village where they saw all the other young elves running about dancing and singing having lots of fun on playing on the swings.

As Alana looked around, she could smell the aroma of sweet strawberries. She glanced around again and noticed that on the trunks of the trees were beautiful carved windows and doors, the overgrown ivy climbing the trees with the giant red daffodils poking through the thick green ivy leafs.

As Alana, lead Thunder through the long red grass holding onto the reins, she felt the hot sun beaming down and warming the soft grass beneath her feet.

Alana and the elf made their way across the grass and were happily greeted by the other very young elflings, eagerly wanting to know all about Alana and her adventures, as El'f bez imeni had taken hold of Thunders reins alongside Flash, within a sudden, Thunder, Flash and Zero had suddenly disappeared in a puff of glittery green smoke. As Alana turned her head and glanced back her eye-catching the green smoke as it disappeared,

"What was that asked Alana?" "I was just sending the horses and zero in the stables," exclaimed El'f bez imeni. "That's so cool" said, Alana, as she carried on walking still holding on to the tiny hands of the elflings, As Alana and the elflings walked across the red grass soon coming to a big old oak tree with big red leafs as they approached the tree one of the little elflings then let's go of Alana's hand running over to the big oak tree with sheer excitement

"Come Alana" she said as she approached the big oak tree.

"Please sit next to me" she beamed, as Alana got a little close she saw the most beautiful little bench carved in the bark of the tree decorated with small carvings of oak trees. As Alana sat between the two elflings.

One of the elflings then, turned to Alana

"Hello so lovely to meet you, my name is Capsuna, and this is my little sister llacuna."

Llacuna had red daisy chain plaits growing in her hair and was slightly smaller than Capsuna, llacuna was also a bit shy and as Alana and the three elves sat laughing having fun and exchanging stories for what seemed like hours, and it was already getting late.

"Come on then," Elf'bez imeni said

"We better go it is nearly time for supper," llacuna suddenly jumped up and shouted

"Yippee it's supper time; is Alana staying for supper," she said with a big smile on her face

"Yes she is," said Elf'bez imeni. Llacuna then holds out her hand

"Come on Alana" she says as Alana holds on to her hand.

Just then, llacuna then starts to run across the red meadow

"We do not want to be late for supper she shouts." As Alana and llacuna enter the red forest with capsuna and Elf'bez imeni not much further behind with the long forest grass beneath their feet, they could hear the birds singing in the treetops, as birds settled down for the evening.

As they then continued to walk through the forest, they soon come to a clearing in the centre of the woods where all the Elves had gathered for supper each one helping with suppertime.
As Alana and the three elves approached the other elves.

Elf'bez imeni then turned to Alana and said

"I would like you to meet elder grandma elf we call her this, as she is one of the oldest elves living here."

"Hello Alana how are you"? It is so good to meet you"

"It's a pleasure to meet you too" said, Alana.
As they both shook hands as Alana and the elder grandma elf stood chatting as llacuna and capsuna were about to come whizzing past.

"Hold on there you two your both filthy" says elder grandma elf as she pulls a face cloth from a big wooden bowl of warm soapy water as elder grandma elf wipes the dirt from their tiny hands and face then she stands looking at them a saying "Off you go now your all nice and clean and ready for supper just please try to stay clean".

"We will stay clean Elder grandma elf" they said together.

Elder grandma elf then turns to Elf'bez imeni

"Please be a dear and go and fetch me some silver berries from the silver town. You can take Alana with you. In addition, please be careful and stay away from older silver elf",

"Of course, I will be careful don't worry I have no intention of going anywhere near older silver elf" she says. In addition, with a little puff of green magic the two horses Thunder and Flash reappear.

Then Alana and Elf'bez imeni climbed on to the horses and galloped towards silver town do not belong shouted Elder grandma elf supper will be ready soon. We will not be long shouted Elf'bez imeni as they rode off towards the edge of the silver town.

Soon they approached silver town Alana sees the huge silver birch trees, which surrounded silver town almost touching the sky with their silver leafs. As they shined in the sunlight from the top of the hill. As they look down onto the town they see the silver rivers silver mountains and silver meadows it is so beautiful says Alana, it is very beautiful says Elf'bez imeni as they both sat on the back of the horses admiring the beauty of silver town then all of a sudden they feel a light breeze.

Just then, the wind started to pick up.

"Older silver elf is up to her tricks again" says Elf be imeni

"What do you mean" says, Alana

"The older silver elf possesses silver magic which is trickery magic",

"Oh dear" said, Alana

"Yes, oh dear indeed we must hurry before everything starts to freeze over".

"It will become Freezing and we will end up being stuck here as the silver magic tricks you into believing that you are stuck here in an ice age like, cold winter and with temperatures so cold that you cannot move just like being frozen in time".

"That sounds so awful" said Alana

"Yes it does that would be awful" said Elf be imeni as they the approached a small silvery lane the lane having the same tall silver birch trees as they had seen coming into silver town. As the horses trotted down the path, they came to a row of small shops carved into the trees.

"This is where we need to be" said Elf be imeni as she claimed down from the horse.

"Come on Alana" she said

"Let's go and get what we need"

"Ok" said, Alana, as they entered the small shop.

"Hello" said Elf keeper.

"Hello" said Elf be imeni

"It's been a long time, mine haven't you grown, and you have brought a friend"

"Yes this is Alana"

"So you're Alana?" Said the Elf keeper

"Indeed I am".

"Well it's a pleasure to meet your acquaintance"

"The pleasure is all mine, nice to meet you too" said Alana.

"Therefore, what will it be today"?

"Just some silver berries please" said Elf'bez imeni.

"Certainly" said Elf keeper as the Elf keeper weighed out the silver berries. As the Elf keeper and Elf'bez imeni began to chat,

"So you are having a party?"

"Yes we are,

"Thought so with asking for the silver berries. It all sounds very nice, hope you have lots of fun"?

"We will thank you."

"By the way, you do know that old Silver Elf is up to her old trickery tricks again"?

"No I did not know that. That will have to be talked about at the next meeting. She is getting way out of control again."

"Anyway, let Elder Grandma Elf know there is a meeting next Thursday in the usual place. In addition, tell Elder Grandma Elf to bring some of her yummy strawberry crumble."

"I will do must be going now and thank you".

"You are most welcome said Elf keeper." As Elf'bez, imeni walks over to the door where Alana is stood looking at all the strange and magical items for sale. Alana then points to one item that has caught her eye.

"What is this strange looking item"? She asks with a puzzled look on her face

"That is a dream catcher it captures every dream ever dreamed."

"Wow that is so fascinating."

"If you are interested I will tell you more about it sometime"?

"That would be great thank you."

"Ok are you ready to ride back to strawberry lagoon"?

"Ready as ever"-said Alana. As Alana and Elf'bez imeni climbed back on to the horses as they gallop down the silvery lane up the hill and back across the red meadow and back to the Elf village at Strawberry lagoon.

Upon their arrival back in strawberry lagoon Elder Grandma Elf greets them.

"Is everything ok"? She smiles.

"Yes thank you" Elder grandma elf, everything is good."

"Elder grandma elf here is your silver berries" as she passes over the bag to Elder grandma elf.

"Thank you"

"You're very welcome."

"Oh and old silver elf was up to her old tricks again and Elf keeper said he would see you at the meeting this Thursday in the usual place, Elf keeper asked if you would take some of your yummy strawberry crumble".

"Will do" she says with a smile.

"I know Elf keeper loves my strawberry crumble said Elder Grandma Elf.

"Come on now supper is ready so don't forget to wash your hands and face".

"We we won't" said Elf be imeni, so Alana and Elf be imeni washed their hands and face in the big wooden bowl of warm soapy water.

Alana and Elf be imeni then walked over to the oak table under the big red oak tree which had carvings of strawberries around the edge. There was a giant strawberry carving in the centre the table. The table was full of big wooden bowls of all kinds of berries, nuts, and loaves of bread filled with fruit and huge jugs of strawberry milk and strawberry coffee and tea and strawberry and kiwi juice.

"This all looks so amazing" said Alana

"You should try some of the pizza it has a cookie dough base, filled with red chocolate pieces that are strawberry flavoured, then layered with strawberry jam and custard. Topped with red banana, red and green kiwi, red pineapple, red star fruit and strawberry pieces"

"I will have some pizza it sounds so yummy says Alana and I will have a drink of Mmmm which one is which"? Asks Alana

"That one's coffee".

"But it is pink"?

"Yes but comes from red coffee beans, and as a unique strawberry flavour".

"That really does sound nice but I think I will have the strawberry milkshake please". Elf'bez imeni then picks up a wooden oak cup and pours Alana a drink as Alana takes a big gulp from the cup.

"That is so rich and creamy it is super yummy."

"Come on let us go, and find somewhere to sit."

As they walk over to the oak trees. On the opposite side from the oak table,

"This seems like a nice place to sit" says Alana.

"Yes, it does" once sat down under the oak tree. Alana puts down the wooden cup by her side and the wooden plate on her lap.

Then takes a big bite from the huge piece of pizza.

"Wow this is so wonderful" Alana says with a mouth full of food.

"Told you" said Elf'bez imeni as they sat munching their pizza Elf'bez imeni then points to the branches on the trees.

"Look at the silver berries"? As Alana looks up

"Wow" she says

"They look so magnificent, like diamond disco lights" as they gleamed in the sunlight.

Then all of sudden the music starts to flow and a familiar song starts to play. The land of make believe.

"I love this song" says Alana

"Well come on then" says Elf' bez imeni let the party begin and let us dance.

After a few minutes of dancing, Alana notices a small boy out of the corner of her eye.

"Who is the little boy"? Alana asks

"I do not know" says Elf'bez imeni.

"However, what I do know is that he is human and from your world".

"He always seems to appear when we have parties and the music is playing."

Just then, Alana starts to walk over to the little boy. She stops suddenly in front of him as his beautiful blue eyes mesmerize her.

"Wow, you have the most beautiful blue eyes" Alana says to the little boy.

However, there was something else about little boy the little boys eyes gave off incredible energy of much warmth and love. As Alana then sits down besides the little boy.

"Hello she says with a big smile.

"Hello Alana" says the little boy.

Then feeling puzzled Alana then asks the little boy,

"How do you know my name?" The boy just winks then smiles. He then leans forward and gives her little kiss on her check then disappears then Alana feels even more puzzled.

As Alana looks up and sees Elf'bez imeni walking towards her. She then tells her about the little boy disappearing

"After awhile he does disappear. So maybe it could be that he woke up in his world that is why he disappeared suddenly."

"Of course" says Alana, you are so right.

"I should have thought that" she says with a smile.

"Anyway come on Alana we must take the horses to the stables they will want their supper".

As they then walk over to one of the oak trees where the horses are grazing.

"Come on Thunder and Flash let us take you to the stables for your supper" said, Alana, as she began to yawn.

"I am starting to feel a little tired" said Alana.

"Me too" said Elf be imeni.

El'f bez imeni also knew that it was nearly time for Alana disappears. She had to get Alana to the stables before sunset in her dream world. Alana then could wake up when the sun was rising in her world.

They then started to walk towards the stables. As Elf bez imeni asks Alana,

"Did you find out anything about the little boy?"

"No, I did not find anything out about him said Alana. He is from my world but not from where I am from."

"I think he is from the east she says,

"But there is one question" said, Alana,

"What is that?" Asked Elf be imeni

"How did he know my name"?

"That I do not know, but what I can tell you that it is not probably the first time you have met. I also do not think it will be the last. Only when the time is right you will see each other again."

"But I have never met him before" said Alana looking puzzled.

"That might be the case for you but he may have been somewhere where you were and seen you. Has you may had not seen him".

"Yes, maybe your right" said Alana.

"I would love to see him again one day he was so sweet."

As they had now arrived at the stables Alana was now feeling really sleepy Elf.bez imeni then turned to Alana.

"Why don't you sit down here?"

"You look really tried you can keep the rabbit company while I feed the horses."

"Ok" said, Alana, as she sat down on the straw next to the bales of hay as the rabbit jump on her lap. As Alana began to cuddle him.

"What's his name"? Asked Alana.

"Riga" said Elf'bez imeni as she could see Alana drifting, into a deep sleep.

As Alana drifted into a deep still cuddling Riga Elf'bez imeni heard her mumble.

"Riga you're so cute" as Alana carried on hugging Riga and with that Alana had disappeared

CHAPTER THREE

As Alana then slowly woke in her own world, a few minutes later cuddled up to her duvet. She then realised that the rabbit Riga was, in fact, was her duvet. As she had one end of the duvet in one hand and slowly rubbing her eye with the other as she began to sit up in bed.

What a wonderful dream thought Alana.

I wonder if I will ever see Elf'bez imeni and the other Elves, again she thought as she looked up at the window. As the sun had started to rise and fill her bedroom with beautiful sunshine. She then began to think about the sweet little boy with the most beautiful blue eyes who had filled her heart with so much love. I must find him again, she said to herself while deep in thought. Then suddenly she hears her mother shout.

"Alana are you up yet"?

"Yes," shouts Alana as she jumps out of bed turns the door handle. As she opens the door, runs downstairs runs across the hallway, and slides across the kitchen floor passed her mum who is preparing her breakfast. She then passes her mother. As her mother shouts after her.

"What about getting dressed and having breakfast"?

"In a minute" shouts Alana

"No now" shouts her mum as Alana runs out the back door and runs down to the bottom of the garden. To see her two ginger and white dutch rabbits Riga and Latvia.

Which Alana had had since she was three years old the rabbits home was magnificent. It was set in the woodland at the bottom of Alana's garden each tree had been carved with windows and doors. When you stood back and looked at it resembled a princess's palace. At the top of the trees, there was thatched roofing the whole area had been designed and developed so that it was safe secure and a natural habit for the rabbits and to keep the natural beauty of the woodland.

As Alana lifted the latch at the side door of the rabbit, run and quickly closing it behind her.

"Hello said, Alana, how are you this morning"? She asked in a soft voice as they both looked up at Alana then both came hopping over to say hello.

"I bet you're ready for some breakfast"? Asked Alana as she gently stroked them. Alana then turns around as she walks over to the large wooden box next to the door she opens the lid and takes out a huge scoop of rabbit musesil as she shares it between the two bowls on the floor she then takes the rabbit bottles which are fixed on to the side of the wooden box empties out the water and then refills them with the tap next to the door.

"There you go" she says stroking both rabbits in turn.

"Must be going now see you later" she says as Alana leaves though the side door Riga and Latvia both glance across and see Alana leave then they carry on munching there breakfast. Alana then shuts the door and closes the latch. Alana then runs back up the garden into the kitchen and asks if her breakfast is ready as she washes her hands and face in the warm soapy water.

"Yes it's been ready for ages and you still need to get dressed, comb your hair and brush your teeth and you are going to be late again for school you cannot be turning up at anytime you want" she said

"Yer well if it was up to me I would roll in school around noon" giggled Alana.

"Yes well is not up to you there is a set time of 8.50 am when you need to be there. If you do not get into a routine now how are you going to manage to hold a job down when you are all grown up?

"I will move to another country in the east" says Alana

"And how's going to help you be on time"? Says her mother.

"Because it's a different time zone" says Alana

"Yes but the East time zone is in front of us" her mother tells her

"Well I will work at night then" after a few seconds of silent's Alana then asks

"Can we travel to the Eastern countries on holiday this year please"?

"Oh not this again we have already been through this before and the answer is still no, I don't know where you get this fascination about the Eastern world from I tell you what when your all grown up, you can pack your bags and move there and I will even buy you the ticket".

"Yay" says Alana swinging here arms in the air, her spoon still in her hand and cornflakes begin flung from her spoon.

"Alana your making a right mess just please go and get ready and go to school".

As Alana rushes upstairs to get ready after about 5 minutes, Alana runs back down the stairs. As she rushes to get her shoes and coat on.

"Ok, I am ready now see you later" as she walks through the kitchen and opens the back door.

"Hang on wait a minute," says her mother as Alana stops at the door as she huffs and puffs.

"You tell me I need to rush because I am going to be late now you're telling me to wait for a minute"

"Because if you have a few spare minutes then you can make sure you have everything." "Like what"? "Asks Alana.

"I have everything"

"What like last Monday? And I had to bring it up to school" as she hands her an envelope

"Oh yes" says Alana

"My dinner money" as she giggles

"Yes your dinner money that reminds me" says Alana

"Can we go Locko Park later to pick strawberries"? "

 "I don't see why not but it will be after tea." Yes that is fine right big hug and kiss and I will see you later see you later."

"Ok," says Alana, as she runs up the driveway, passed the front of her house through the housing estate across the field passed the brook. And says Hello to the two horses grazing in the field as she passes by. She then turns the corner under the trees and down through the school gates as she passes the other children still coming through the gates of the school. Alana runs along the path between the classes' rooms and the grass area on the opposite side with the trees hanging over the fence. Alana carries on until she gets to the playground and stops for a second by the two benches as she looks around then spots her friends who beckon her to go over to where they are playing.

"Did you have a good weekend"? "Asks Alana

"Yes I did I went the park on Saturday," says Heather.

 "I did too I played out and rode my bike," Tracey said.

"I was watching the television till my mum cut the plug off."

"Why did your mum do that"? "Alana asked Lisa in a fit of giggles.

 "Because my mum had told us to keep the volume down and we didn't listen," she said,

"Oh dear," said Alana

"But its funny" she giggled.

"So what was your watching at the time," asked Tracey, as she tried to stop laughing

"Super Gran," she said

"I watched that as well," said Tracey

"Its really very funny yes," said Lisa.

"So what did you do at the weekend Alana," asked her friends.

"I stayed at my grandma and granddads house for the weekend my grandma had taken me swimming on Saturday morning. Then in the afternoon, we went on one of those mystery coach tours. On Sunday we had roast dinner and strawberry crumble and custard"

"That sounds so yummy we love crumble and custard" said her friends.

Just then, the school bell rang as Alana and her friends walked to their classroom. Once they were all sat down at their tables. The teacher then takes the register after the register and all the dinner money was collected. It was time for assembly in the school hall where all the children sang hymns.

Then afterwards the children all returned to their classrooms all ready for lessons as all the children sat down. The Teacher then spoke as she handed a piece of plain paper to each child.

"I want you to draw your favourite moment from the weekend then I will get each one of you to tell the rest of the class about your picture." The children then set to work on their pictures as the Teacher sat at her desk as she finished some paperwork. After a while, the Teacher asked if everyone had finished all the children agreed, they had.

"Ok" said the Teacher as one by one each child spoke and showed their picture of their favourite moment from the weekend then came Alana's turn. She explained this strawberry lagoon with a smile.

"So where is this strawberry lagoon"? "Asked her Teacher.

"As I have never heard of such a place".

"It was a place from my dream," she said.

"So it is not a real moment from your weekend," said the Teacher. Handing Alana another plain piece of paper

"I want you to draw something from the real world, not from a dream world," she said

"But it is real," said Alana feeling upset and trying not to cry. As the Teacher said,

"You're always away with the fairies" No they were elves," she said cheekily

"Living in a dream world will get you nowhere," the Teacher said as she walked away.

Just then, the school bell rang for playtime. The classroom emptied very quickly as Alana still feeling upset slowly walked out of the classroom looking at the floor and dragging her feet slowly. Arriving at the playground as she stood alone. She then heard her friends shout

"Come on Alana" as she looked up all the children were sitting on the grass at the top of the playground all waiting for her. As Alana walked up to the top of the playground and on to the grass. There one of the children asked.

"Please tell us all about strawberry lagoon",

"Of course, I will" she said with a big smile on her face. Alana then told the children all about her adventures in strawberry lagoon how she came to be there. In addition, when she meets Elf'bez imeni under the red willow tree. She told them about the golden river, elder grandma elf. The two elflings capsuna and Ilsuna. Silver town the Elf keeper, Older silver Elf and all the strawberry flavoured food. Her friends and classmates hanging on every word.

"Thank you for sharing your dream of strawberry lagoon with us they" said as they headed back to their classroom.

"Please tell us more dreams again soon."

"I will," said Alana, as she was feeling so happy and excited that her friends and classmates wanted to hear all about her adventures in her dreams.

As the weeks months and years passed by Alana continued to tell her friends and classmates all about her adventures in her dream world. She told them about the singing bluebells and ballet dancing with the bluebell fairies in the evergreen forest. The sunlight rays that filled the forest with enchanted magic. She told them about the lonely beach where the sand was pure white the colour of the sea was a midnight purple. Where beautiful purple butterflies with silver edged wings would flutter by leaving a trail of silver stars as she sunbathed for hours. The lavish fairytale princess a party she attended and as time passed Alana was growing up fast her dreams had started to change. However, a first Alana did not notice, as the changes were only small as Alana was now 12 years old but still loved to dream about fairytale worlds. Still be as much a part of them as she was a few years ago. She never gives up hope of returning to strawberry lagoon to see the Elves and finding the little boy with the most beautiful blue eyes from strawberry lagoon as she still desperately searched her dreams to find him.

CHAPTER FOUR

It was now the summer of 1987. Alana had been out roller-skating with some friends one Friday evening, having returned home in the late evening feeling a little hungry. Decided to have some supper, after eating a bowl of cereal and drinking a mug of hot honey flavoured chocolate and marshmallows. Goes upstairs brushes her teeth and hair, then changes into her nightdress and climbs into her bed within minutes Alana was sound asleep.

A few moments later she found herself back, in a place she knew all too well as. Alana stood up and glanced around smiling, as it had been a little while since she was last here well that's what she thought, as she remembered all the fond memories while walking over to the bedroom door the door seemed different it seemed old and worn that's so strange thought, Alana I never noticed the door being old looking before as she then turned the handle and opened the door Oh well thought Alana it was probably like that all the time just never noticed it then Alana walked across the landing and headed for the top of the stairs when she arrived at the top of the stairs she looked around and noticed the dust across the landing and down the stairs there were cobwebs hanging from the ceiling her palace seemed drab and cold.

Alana then walked down the staircase and across the marble floor. The palace seemed lifeless like, as nobody had been there for a very long time.

Alana slowly walked over to the patio doors. Alana could see ivy vines climbing through the edges of one of the doors. Which was closed the other door open only slightly and hanging off its hinges Alana then stood in front of the doors. She then looked up and down at the doors this really does not seem right. She mumbled to herself, as it must have only been a month or two since I was last here she thought. Alana then reached forward as she tried to push open the door further but it would not budge. So Alana decided to pull the door rather than push and managed to open the door just enough for her to squeeze through then as she slides halfway through the gap of the door she the noticed a tree growing across the patio doors.

She looked around; the ground was all-soggy and as the fog began to thicken rather quickly. Alana stood between the door and the tree debating whether she should climb up and over or crawl under the tree. There were thick ivy vines and brambles twisted around. The tree growing up the walls windows and doors as Alana looked around she noticed something usual but very familiar with the brambles the trees and vines they all had a silver tint. That is weird she thought as she began to climb the tree. However, it was too difficult to climb as the wet soggy bark made it difficult for her to climb. She then began to crawl under the tree Alana could see a large open grassed area all I need is to get there then I can go and look for thunder flash and zero she said to herself it was not far but it was tough trying to crawl under and through the thick brambles and ivy vines as she finally crawled out on the grass.

Alana then lay on her back with cuts scratches and bruises looking up at the sky.

"Wow" she said in an exhausted tone as she could see the sun was shining and not a cloud in the sky as she slowly turned her head to look across from where her palace had once been visible she noticed a huge black cloud hanging over the palace and within a few minutes all Alana could see was a sheet of thick silvery fog and she could no longer see the palace the thick brambles the trees or the ivy vines.

"Oh dear, my wonderful palace in rack and ruins". She sobs as she covered her face with her hands as she shook her head after a few minutes she decided that she must press on.

Alana was feeling sad about her palace as she looked over to where the fog had hidden her dream home. Thinking about what she should do about it then. Alana thought that she could not do it on her own. I need someone to help me so I will have to come and sort this out later as I need to find Thunder, Flash and Zero still sitting on the grass she sees the country lane that she often used to ride up and down with Thunder flash and Zero. I must find them Alana thought as she started to walk down the lane. As she began to look around this all looks the same as it has always done she thought, as she started too walked down the lane.

Alana could smell the fresh scent of the meadow flowers growing under the hedgerows she could hear the honey bees buzzing as they collected their nectar from the sweet-smelling meadow flowers the birds singing high up in the treetops.

Sometime later she suddenly stops and looks over her shoulder for one last look. She could still see the big black cloud over the dense silvery fog. Then as Alana was about to carry on walking she spots a little white country cottage out the corner of her eye that is so strange. I never seen this little cottage before and decides to get a closer look as she walks over to the little white picket fence which surrounds the cottage things start to seem very strange indeed. Alana places her hands on the on the top of the fence as she pulls herself up she soon notices the frost and snow covering the small garden of the cottage the trees frozen solid the silver framed windows covered in icicles.
The frost crept up the windows how very strange thought Alana how can this be the sun is shining and it's a hot summers day as she looked around she could not see snow or ice anywhere else. Surely in this heat the snow and ice should have melted away thought Alana this place is starting to give me the chills as she climbs down off the fence and continues to walk down the lane.

A little while later, she comes to a crossroads. This is new to me I have ridden up and down this lane many times and never seen a crossroads here before, then she notices something even more bizarre a wooden signpost with no places or directions on. Therefore, which way do I go she wondered after a few minutes of debating she just carries on in the same direction as she had already been walking?

Alana then comes to a forest area where she hears the sound of running water.

"Just what I need I could do with a drink I am so thirsty and it's so hot." As she wipes her forehead with her hand, she then takes a detour from the lane and walks through the beautiful evergreen forest. With the fresh smell of pine as she pulls, back the branches of the trees she sees a beautiful rainbow waterfall, where the water, falls as long flowing rainbows.

"Oh, my" she gasps.

"I have never seen anything as magnificent as this before" as she walks over to the edge of the waterfall. Alana then bends down as she holds her hands together as she then scopes up some water. As she tastes the water.

"Yum," she says as she scopes another hand full of water. It tastes like a fruit cocktail she thought to herself. As she then stood up and walked down the side of the rainbow river as she went off to explore the curious place.

Having not walked far Alana spots an apple tree. This tree has rainbow effect leaves how beautiful as she looks at the tree with a smile with different coloured apples do not mind if I do as she picks an apple from the tree. Then giving it a rub on her top takes a big bite from the yellow apple.

"Wow" its tastes of sherbet lemons and so juicy.

"I wonder what the other apples taste like." as she picks a shiny black Apple.

"This one tastes of black cherry ice cream and tastes so good." After finishing her apples Alana decides to carry on exploring, some more as Alana walks a little further. Alana comes to a rainbow coloured stone bridge. Alana starts to walk across the bridge and stops in the middle to admire the beautiful rainbow waterfall.

As she is watching the waterfall, she notices the rainbow butterflies fluttering close to the water as they played. There so pretty she thought. After a while she continued walking across the bridge. As Alana wanted to take a closer look at the butterflies, Alana continued to walk along the bridge and on to the rainbow coloured grass and down the side of the waterfall to get a closer look. Alana then heard a someone say

"Hello, Alana, how are you?" It has been a long time.

"Who said that," said Alana as she looked around and not being able to see anyone as she stood looking puzzled. Alana then heard someone say,

"Alana, it's me I am over here," said a familiar sounding voice as she looked back at the butterflies and the rainbow waterfall

"Hang on one sec and stay there," said the voice as a beautiful butterfly flew over her and landed on the grass. Within seconds, the butterfly had transformed.

"Hello Alana" said Elf' bez imeni

"Hi said Alana looking quite stunned" as Elf' bez imeni gave her a big hug.

"It has been a long while and you don't look any older, but you seem older if that makes sense" said Elf be imeni.

"It sure does said, Alana I know exactly what you mean and it's so wonderful to see you again."

"It's so good to see you" said Elf is imeni.

"I did try to find you and strawberry lagoon again said Alana but never found it again."

"Maybe there is a reason why you found it the first time, and maybe you will find it again when the time is right and maybe just maybe you might found strawberry lagoon when you are not even looking for it, and you least expect it".

"I really do hope" so said, Alana

"Hopefully I will return to strawberry lagoon again one day."

"I am sure you will," Alana, and Elf' bez imeni then sat together on the edge of the rainbow river as they splashed the water with their feet reminiscing about the wonderful time they had in strawberry lagoon.

Elf' bez imeni then asked Alana.

"How did you get those cuts and scratches"?

"When I woke up in my palace things seemed very different and I had to crawl under vines and brambles which I caught myself on many times then my palace disappeared under a thick silvery fog."

"How interesting" said El'f bez imeni?

"As there have been some strange happenings here too it all started sometime ago just after you left Elder grandma elf disappeared and has not been seen since."

"Why what happened"?

"It all started when she went down into silver town to buy an item from Elf keeper but never arrived we do think that older silver Elf has had something to do with her disappearance"

"That so awful" said, Alana

"And while we are on the subject of things disappearing I cannot find Thunder, Flash, or Zero anywhere"

"You have just reminded me that I had something to tell you a few months ago it was the strangest thing Thunder, Flash and Zero just appeared one day out of nowhere in strawberry lagoon and they are safe and well and we the Elves are taking care of them so do not worry I would use the green magic to bring them here but then I would not have enough for me and the other Elves to return to Strawberry lagoon as we are running low on green magic as it is Elder grandma elf that makes the green magic this is why we have come here to try to find Elder grandma elf and we had to disguise our self's as butterflies so we would not be seen if Older silver elf is lurking about and spots us".

"There will be trouble"

"Ok I understand, I also did wonder why you were disguised as a butterfly when you had transformed into you" said Alana.

"So have you been here before"? Asked Alana.

"What here at Rainbow falls?"

"I have been here many times but things are going wrong the rainbow coloured water is not as bright as it once was and Animals, Items and everyone has been placed in places they should not be" said Elf bez imeni.

"So what are we going to do to restore everything back to normal"?

"Yes"

"And you can start by getting me home as I do not belong here" said a sad voice as Alana and Elf bez imeni both turned their heads to see behind them. As they looked over to where the rainbow coloured conifer trees, was stood a golden unicorn.

"What are you doing in rainbow falls"? Asked Elf bez imeni. As she excitedly ran over to see her friend.

"I am not sure I had gone to take a nap and I woke up here a few weeks ago. I was really confused. I just want to get home to Golden River"

"It is going to be ok said Alana and I will help you"

"Thank you so much"

"It is my pleasure by the way this is Alana. Alana this is Jin jiao ma he is from Golden River in strawberry lagoon and I am sure that older silver elf has something to do with this."

"I am certain that she had something to do with it to, she is such a meddling menace" said Jin jiao ma.

"That is so true she defiantly needs to be stopped" said Elf' bez imeni.

"But where do we start looking" said Alana,

"I am not sure but let's go on an adventure and see where it takes us that way we may find some clues along the way" said Elf' bez imeni.

"That's so Awesome and sounds so exciting a new adventure come on then what we waiting for she said excitedly" as Alana then started to walk towards the evergreen forest on the edge of Rainbow falls.

"Can we go this way through the trees as I want to show you this little cottage I saw coming down the lane just on the other side of these trees" said Alana.

"Ok it is as good as anywhere to make a start on our adventure. But first let us get some supplies from the apple tree" said Elf' bez imeni.

"Yes let's get some delicious apples for our journey. I tried the black apple and a yellow one and both are very delicious" said Alana.

"Well you should try the red and blue apples."

"Why what flavour are they"?

"The red ones are strawberry lemonade and the blue ones are bubble gum flavour."

"Wow they sound so yummy" as Alana picked a red and blue apple.

"Mmm I think I will have a red and blue apple as well and what about you Jin jiao ma which apples would you like"?

"I would like a black and a green apple please." As Alana stood tip toed to reach a big shiny green apple.

"What flavour is this one"? She said as she handed it to Elf' bez imeni.

"Its lemon and lime flavour and very juicy"

"It sounds wonderfully yummy"

"It is said Jin jiao ma and my favourite apple too you should try the white ones some time their vanilla cream flavour"

"I certainly will do one day" Alana said.

"Come on then shall we go and see the cottage you want to show us"?

"Yes indeed," as they walked through the evergreen trees and came out on the lane that Alana knew so well.

"Which way do we go"? Asked Elf' bez imeni.

"That way" as she pointed up the lane.

"Ok let us get going then." As the three friends started to walk up the lane together as the sun shone down on them. However, it was not as hot as it had been when Alana had first walked down the lane earlier in the day.

It was now late afternoon and so much cooler than it had been when Alana walked down the lane a few hours before. After a few minutes, Alana stopped and picked some flowers growing in the grass on the side of the lane. After picking the flowers, she looked up and saw that her friends had walked quite far ahead in front. Alana then ran to catch up with her friends who had been chatting as they walked and not realised that Alana had stopped to pick some flowers. As soon as Alana caught up with her friends she said to Elf' bez imeni.

"I have a little gift for you" as she handed her the bunch of flowers to El'f bez imeni.

"Flowers for me?"

".There so beautiful thank you so much" as Elf' bez imeni sniffed the flowers.

"They smell so wonderful."

"They are forget-me-nots."

"Perfect as I will never forget you" she giggled. As the three friends were about to carry on walking when Elf' bez imeni noticed the wooden signpost.

That's the strangest signpost I have ever seen it has eight different signs and only tells you the directions for rainbow falls."

"That's odd as there were no places listed on there when I first noticed it earlier today."

"That's even more strange that a place had suddenly appeared after you had found it" said Elf' bez imeni.

"Yes indeed it is strange" and as Alana and Elf' bez imeni continued to chat about the strangeness of the sign post Jin jiao ma then nudged Alana. As he then asked

"Is that the cottage you where talking about"? As Alana looked up the lane and in the distance could see the cottage she had told her friends about.

"Yes it is the cottage I want to show you" she said.

So as the three friends then carried on their journey walking quickly towards the cottage, but as the three friends continued to walk along the lane the lane became steeper like they were walking up a hill and the cottage always remaining in the distance and on the horizon. The more they walked the more the lane became steeper.

"This is all very peculiar as this lane has always been flat there was never a hill here before."

"That really is weird a steep hill were there was not one before said Elf' bez imeni, as she looked at Alana confused that really does not make sense, and we have been walking for hours and we don't seem to get any closer, it always seems that the cottage is no nearer and no further away"

"You know what I think" said Jin jiao ma.

"What" said Alana and Elf' bez imeni at the same time.

"We should sit and eat our apples."

"I think we need to rest for a little while"

"That really does sound like a good idea" said Elf 'bez imeni as the three friends sat munching their apples as they chatted about the lane what had become a steep hill and the little cottage.

"I am sure that it is that lunatic Elf that is causing all this mischief" said Jin jiao ma.

"I think so too" said Elf' bez imeni as she stood up.

"Ok, are we ready to make a move then" she said as she peered over the wall that ran up the hill.

"We are high up here she said and the view is so beautiful I can see right across the land".

"Come and see"

"Coming" said Alana and Jin jiao ma as they joined Elf' bez imeni at the wall to see the beautiful views. Then as Alana placed her hands on the wall to get a better look she realised that she had placed her hands on top of some wood. Which was over grown with honeysuckle she then pushed back the over growing honeysuckle and then realised it was a wooden gate as she pushed hard on the wood at the top the gate flung open.

"Let's try this way" Alana said excitedly as she walked on to the steep hill on the other side of the gate as Elf' bez imeni and Jin jiao ma then followed Alana though the gate.

"I thought we were going to see this cottage you wanted to show us" said Elf' bez imeni,

"Yes I know I still want to show you the cottage, if we go this way it may lead us to a different route."

"Ok let's try this way then so the three friends started to walk down the hill hoping to find another route to the cottage as they carried on walking down hill though the over grown grass with the sweet smelling meadow flowers and the late afternoon summer breeze. The three friends continued to walk down the hill suddenly a cold strong gust of wind blew straight though them. Alana began to shiver.

"That wind has got a cold nip" she said.

"It does seem to be getting colder" said Elf' bez imeni as they hurried down the hill with not much further to go.

Soon the three friends reached a fast flowing river, which stretched right round the bottom of hill.

"And how do you suppose we get across" said Elf' bez imeni.

"Over here shouted" Jin jiao ma as both Alana and Elf' bez imeni looked over to where Jin jiao ma was crossing on the stepping stones.

"You be careful" shouts Elf' bez imeni.

"I am always careful" as he jumped from one stone to another as Elf bez imeni covered her eyes with her hands.

"Well he made it across" said Alana.

"Are you sure" she said.

"Yes very sure" as she moved her hands from her eyes.

"Come on then it is our turn to cross"

"But it does not look safe" said Elf' bez imeni.

"You will be absolutely fine let's link arms and jump together" said Alana.

"Ok thank you" said Elf'bez imeni as Alana and Elf' bez imeni jumped from stone to stone within a few minutes they had crossed over the river. Once across the river Alana stood in the long grass as she gazed around a swarm of ladybirds spiralled up and around her as she spun around.

"This is wonderful she" said to El'f bez imeni as the swarm of ladybirds began to fly across the meadow and soon disappeared into the distance.

"That was so amazing they keep tickling my face with their feet as the flew up into the sky"

"You're so funny" said Elf' bez imeni as she fell about laughing.

"What's so funny"? Asked Alana.

"The fact that the ladybirds were tickling your face" she said.

"Actually, it is quite funny" she said as Alana and Elf' bez imeni stood chatting and giggling about the ladybirds.

Just then Jin jiao ma interrupted then.

"Do you hear some music coming from the woods"? All three of them began to listen.

"I do hear music" said Elf' bez imeni.

"So do I" said Alana.

"Come on let's go and see who is playing the music" said Jin jiao ma.

"Ok" they all agreed as they started to walk towards the woods and closer to where the music was coming from as they entered the woods they soon realised where the music was coming from the bluebell fairies were having a party.

"Hello Alana nice to see you again" said bluebell delicious.

"So lovely to see you again".

"It has been such a long time since I last seen you Elf' bez imeni and you to Jin jiao ma".

"So you having a party" said Alana.

"Yes said bluebell delicious.

"It is bluebell marshmallows birthday today"

"Wonderful I love party's especially birthday parties" said Alana.

"Would you like a drink"? Asked bluebell delicious.

"Yes please" said Alana. The bluebell fairy then handed her a giant bluebell.

"There you are said bluebell delicious" as Alana sipped the drink.

"This is so yummy" said Alana.

"What is it"? She asked.

"Bluebell wine" she said.

"Wine? But I am not older enough to be drinking wine" she said.

"It is not real wine" said bluebell delicious.

"It is more of a fruit juice than a wine."

"Well it is very nice anyway."

"So let's get this party swinging" she said. Alana then began to look around she noticed a familiar face sat under a tree. She then slowly stared to walk over to the tree.

"Hello again said Alana.

"Hello Alana" said the little boy.

"It's so good to see you again too" as Alana sat down beside the little boy under the green maple tree as they both drank their bluebell wine from the giant bluebells.

"This is super sweet" said the little boy.

"Yes it is said Alana but very yummy indeed".

"Indeed" said the little boy.

As Alana and the little boy drank from there giant bluebells Alana began to feel sleepy. As she began to talk to the little boy.

"You still have not told me how you know my name, and most importantly why won't you tell me your name"? without saying anything the little boy just grinned at Alana as she yawned, her words began to sound slurred as she drifted off into a deep sleep underneath the maple tree as she gently woke from her sleep and rubbed her eyes.

CHAPTER FIVE

As Alana's mother stood in the doorway of her bedroom as Alana was just waking.

"Good morning Alana"? She said.

"You were talking in your sleep again"

"Yes well I was having such a wonderful dream" said Alana with a giggle and a smile.

"Really said her mother"

"I would never have guessed anyway are you getting up now as I can drop you off at your grandma and granddad's house in the village if you still want to go. However, you will have to be ready in about 30 minutes."

"Ok said Alana jumping out of her bed I will be ready I love going to grandma and granddad's house". She beamed as she ran into the bathroom and turned on the shower.

"Well ok shouted her mum do you want me to do you some breakfast or will you have some when you get to grammar and granddad's house."

"I will be down in 5 minutes for breakfast can I have rice krispies please"? Shouted Alana.

"OK" shouts her mum as she goes downstairs after getting ready Alana runs downstairs and goes into the kitchen and sits down at the table The table already been laid with her rice krispies poured into her bowl with a jug of milk freshly squeezed orange juice two slices of toast cut into triangles just how Alana likes it to have breakfast.

After breakfast Alana goes off upstairs to brush her teeth, as she is brushing her teeth Alana hears her mum shouts upstairs to Alana.

"Hurry up we should have left like 5 minutes ago"

"Coming" Alana shouts as she quickly spits out the toothpaste and wipes her mouth with the cloth. Seconds later Alana runs down stairs grabbing her coat off the coat peg and shoes of the rack as she hurry's out though the kitchen and out the back door and up the driveway to her mum waiting in the car, as her mum opens the passenger door. "Have you locked the back door behind you"?

"No I have not I thought you had" she says

"How can I have locked the door"?

"When I am in the car waiting for you and you came out the door last" "Oh yer" she giggles

"Well please go lock the door the keys are already in the lock"

"Ok" as she throws her shoes and coat on the front seat and runs down the driveway and locks the back door as she walks back to the passenger side of the car, opens the door and moves her shoes and coat of the seat. As her mum yells

"Come on Alana we need to get going you don't half mess about I am already late for work" as Alana clips in her seat belt as her mum starts to drive off and around the corner as her mum tells Alana

"I will pick you up from grandmas and granddads a few hours just after lunch"

"Oh I wanted to stay longer"

"Well then you will have to make your own way home"

"Ok that's fine said Alana I may just stay over if that's OK"?

"Of course that's OK with me" said her mum. "But you will have to check if that's OK with your grandma and granddad and what about your nightwear and fresh clothes"

"Oh that's ok I have a plenty in my room at Grandmas and Granddads. As they were still talking they approached the village driving over the toll bridge they stop to pay the toll they then carry on driving under the waterfall lightly feeling the spray of the water on their faces through the windows of the car as they drive up the hill and then they pull up outside grandmas and granddads cottage.

Alana then gets out of the car.

"Don't forget your shoes her mum shouts after her."

"I have them" says Alana as she shuts the car door and says bye to her mum.

"Hope work goes ok"? Say Alana

"Thank you and don't forget to say hello grandma and granddad for me as can't come in as I am late for work will you tell them I will see them later" with that mum speeds away Alana comes up to the gate in front of the cottage as she walks into the garden its full of an awry of colourful and sweet smelling flowers full in bloom reminding her of her dreams as she walks up the path under the arch with the flowers growing across a wooden arch and all around the out skirts of the garden grew big conifers which her granddad had planted years before Alana was born so that her granddaughter could enjoy them as she grew up and got older. And also help granddad with the gardening.
She was so happy to be with her grandparents.
As they loved listening to all her stories of her dreams and many adventures she had been on but I think deep down they knew she was not lying an truly believed what their granddaughter was telling them was real as far as they were concerned. As Alana walk up the three steps the door opened before she good that chance to knock as her grandma had been watching for her to arrive.

"Your mum has gone quickly" as she put her arms around Alana to give her a cuddle and a kiss.

"Mum said she is late for work and will see you around lunch time" oh and i would like to stay if i can until mum gets back from work or stay for the weekend that's sounds lovely I would love you to stay for the weekend so what we got planned for today gardening or listening to me and my stories from my dreams or some baking? "

"So what would you like to do today asked grandma I would like to make some gingerbread if that's ok of course it's ok said, grandma.

"Then we could cut the gingerbread into elves," said Alana

"That sounds like a wonderful idea" said, grandma.

"Come on then" said grandma. Let's get started now and they will be ready for lunchtime then you can give your mum one to try"

"She will love that" said Alana with a big grin on her face. As she eagerly ran into the kitchen feeling excited as she starts to get all of the ingredients out of the baking cupboard.

"Come then grandma I have got all the ingredients out" Hang on one minute" she said "let me just get the recipe book and I will need to pre heat the oven"

"Ok said Alana as she arranged all the ingredients on the table and fetched out the mixing bowls scales and spoons ready to make her gingerbread Elves as Alana stood waiting. Grandma soon found the recipe book. "Here you are Alana" as she passed the recipe book over to her.

"The ginger bread recipe in this book is the best."

"Thank you grandma" said Alana

"You're very welcome now then do you need any help or are you going to make them on your own"

"I just need you to melt me some butter if that's ok that's absolutely fine" as grandma gets out a pan and turns on the hob on the cooker as grandma then began to gently melt the butter on the stove and Alana began weighing out the ingredients.

As Alana then began to tell her grandma about her latest dream while she made the gingerbread elves and how she meets up with El'f bez imeni again.

As Alana told her grandma that her palace was in rack and ruin and the palace was disappearing in the silvery fog and how distraught she felt and how things had changed.

How her dreams were not as beautiful and sweet as they once were and how she could see on the horizon all the perfect places she once loved but could no longer reach them and the beautiful little boy with the amazing blue eyes she got to see again and still longed to find out his name as Alana's grandma sat at the table as she listened carefully to what Alana had to say.

Alana stood cutting out her gingerbread elves as Alana's grandma listened to Alana talk about her dreams which she always found fascinating.

"I don't know what has change but things seem so different in my dreams than they did a few months ago" said Alana with huff as her grandma noticed Alana's eyes started to look sad as she know that Alana always had amazing dreams and loved making new friends throughout her dreams.

As Grandma put the green gingerbread elves in the oven to cook she sat down at the table and pulled over a chair.

"Come and sit down my darling Alana" she said as Alana sat down next to her grandma. Grandma then began to speak softly.

"Alana my dear you have always had such wonderful dreams and your dreams are part of your journey of life and so much a part of who you are and certainly you will continue to have many more amazing adventures with your friends in strawberry lagoon and many more places and where ever your dreams take you so please do not feel sad."

"The reason your dreams are changing is that you're now in your teens and growing up fast. Your hormones are starting to kick in.
This is why your dreams are becoming strange and messed up.
But do not worry it won't be forever.
I do think that at the moment that older silver elf is feeding off your hormones. It is making her more and more powerful as you have become more vulnerable.
The more vulnerable you become older silver elf will become even stronger you can use this to your advantage.
In time you will become more powerful than older silver elf over time you find you will that you have all the power to make your dreams more beautiful than ever and rise up against older silver elf.
You need to round up all friends and fight the evil forces in your with the good your dreams may seem to get worse at the moment but they will get better trust me said, grandma, as Alana stood up thank you grandma as she gave her a big hug that's what grandmas are here for. It will be ok" said, grandma.

"Thank you grandma" said Alana as she gave her a big hug.

"Your welcome" said her grandma

"Come now we better check the gingerbread as its been in there about 20mins".

"The gingerbread elves should be ready now as she walks over to the oven and gently opens the oven a whoosh of sweet smelling ginger bread filled the kitchen.

"Wow grandma said they defiantly smell ready to me what you think Alana"?

"Oh yes there defiantly done"

"Ok I will let them cool down awhile and then we can decorate them." So while the gingerbread elves are cooling you can get on with making the icing" said grandma.

"There are plenty of different food colours in the pantry for making them look more elves like" "Thank you grandma."

"What colours do you want says grandma green and red" says Alana.

"With some sparkly bits" then grandma took out some grease proof paper and stencilled out some elf ears with the icing. By now the gingerbread had cooled enough to decorate as Alana began to decorate the gingerbread elves.
As grandma told her it was nearly time for lunch.

"What would you like on your sandwiches"?

"Jam please" said Alana.

"What flavour would you like"? Asked grandma as she open the cupboard door there was dozens of flavours to choose from. As Alana peered around and looking at all the jams with delight as she picked up one. And held it in her hand as she looked at the label and read out the flavour of the jam.

"Blueberry and custard"?

"Where do you get all these strange flavours of jam from"? Asked Alana.

"I make them you should try the blueberry and custard one it's very nice" said her grandma

"No thanks maybe another time" said Alana.

"I think I will stick to just plain strawberry jam."

"Ok" as her grandma reaching in the cupboard and handed Alana the strawberry jam as Alana hand her grandma the blueberry and custard jam back.
After a little while having eaten there sandwiches there was a knock at the door as Alana ran to answer it.

"Hello Alana" said her mother.

"Grandma is in the kitchen" as her mother walks through the hall and in to the kitchen.

"Look mum I and grandma have made some gingerbread elves."

"Very nice Alana" says her mother.

"Would you like one"?

"Yes please I will take one to have after my supper."

"So Alana is you coming home tonight or are you staying with grandma and granddad"? I

"Am staying here tonight is that ok grandma"?

"Of course it is" said grandma.

Where's your granddad I thought he was of work this week"? Asked Alana's mother.

"Granddad is of work this week he has gone to Manchester to fetch is mother."

"Yay great grandma is coming to stay I am glad I am staying here" said Alana excitedly.

"Well they won't be back till tomorrow morning"

"Ok then I am going so you can get ready for great grandma coming and I will see you tomorrow" as she open the door as Alana and grandma wave her goodbye. With that grandma turned to Alana and said.

"After supper it's early to bed"

"Ok" grandma.

"I will run you a bath and here put a gingerbread elf under your pillow then you will have sweet dreams of elves."

Chapter SIX

That evening after a nice hot soak in the bath with her favourite blueberry bubble gum bubble bath and her hot chocolate and marshmallows.

Alana soon got snuggled up in bed thinking about the wonderful day she had with grandma baking green gingerbread elves and thinking about what grandma had told her as she slowly drifted into a deep sleep not forgetting what grandma had told her and finding herself back in the grounds of her palace with the fog thicker more dense and much colder than it was when she was last there. Also the last time Alana saw El'f bez imeni we had such a magical time she thought. Oh, I do hope I bump into her today as it has been ages since I have seen her.

This fog is so ridicules It just seems to be getting thicker and I can no longer see the palace as the fog is to thick to see my way if El'f bez imeni was here she would know what to do as Alana became increasingly more uncomfortable in a palace she once felt so happy and contented but as she began to turn to look around Alana began to notice the darkness on the horizon creeping ever much more closer making Alana feel a little on edge something is coming she thought. I can sense it as the wind began to howl she felt a shiver down her spine.

Alana stood having no idea as to where to go or what to do with herself she soon caught a glimpse of figure flickering in the fog and what looked like the figure carrying a lamp. Alana began to slowly to take a few steps to get a closer look as she stepped closer and closer. Suddenly the air began to smell of something tasty as Alana crept closer as she slowly walked thought the cold fog. She notice the outlines of the trees as the light lit up the fog it really is so cold she thought as she walked with folded arms and rubbing her arms with her hands.

"I wish I had worn something warmer" she said. Just wearing my thin silk night gown is not good. I just hope I do not catch a chill.

Then as Alana looked straight ahead through the thick fog she saw the outline of the trees with lamps hanging on the branches. And a familiar figure stood at a stone table with a big wooden cauldron as the figure using a large ladle to feed a large gathering of figures stood around the stone table as the fog began to get thicker as Alana could barely see who or what was in front. Then as Alana approached the stone table she looked at the familiar figure Alana's face lit up with a big smile.

"Hello elder grandmas Elf how are you"?

"Oh my" said Elder grandma elf

"How are you Alana" as she placed the large ladle down and gave Alana a huge hug.

"Wow you have grown so much and I have really missed you"

"I have missed you too" said Alana.

"It has been such a long time"

"It has indeed" said elder grandma elf

"Is El'f bez imeni here" asked Alana as she looked around

"No she is not I have not seen her for a while" said elder grandma elf.

"Come let's have a chat so I can fill you in to what's been happening here"

"Ok said Alana.

"Would you like some of my homemade soup"?

"What flavour is the soup asked Alana leaning over the big wooden cauldron as the steam warmed her face?

"The soup is lemon, elderflower, and carrot sorry it is only basic"

"I will have some it smells and sounds lovely and sometimes basic is best" as elder grandma elf ladled some soup into a large wooden bowl as elder grandma elf beckoned over another elf.

"Do you mind just serving the soup for a little while"?

"Ok that's not a problem elder grandma elf thank you Capsuna".

"Capsuna said Alana how are you long time no see" as Capsuna looked up Alana she screeched in excitement.

"How are you it is so good to see you"

"You too"

"Are you going to stay for a while"?

"Hopefully" said Alana

"Ok I will come and have a chat with you shortly" said Capsuna.

"Ok I will come and catch up with you for a chat" said Alana

"Come said elder grandma elf lets go and sit over there at one of those stone tables." There was a row of stone tables in a straight line opposite where the soup was being served as they sat down elder grandma elf passed Alana a wooden plate piled high with bread.

"Thank you" Alana said as she grabbed a piece of bread from the plate. Alana then started to dip the bread into the soup as she asked elder grandma elf

"Why are the elves where here in a dark foggy forest handing out bread and soup and not in strawberry lagoon"?

"Us elves have fallen on hard times we cannot return to strawberry lagoon as we do not have the ingredients to make any more green magic for us to travel back home".

"We have become destitute. We do not have much of a variety of food here and the elves and fairies are struggling and they are so hungry so they come here for food and some come from very far away I have seen some who have travelled for days with nothing to eat just to come and get soup and bread and some are very thin"

"That's awful said Alana with tears in her eyes when I last saw El'f bez imeni she said things were going wrong. I did not think it was this bad so how did it get to this"? Asked Alana.

"Well it happened sometime ago. I was on my way to silver town to see elf keeper. As I needed to discuss the mischief that older silver elf was causing. As I walked down the hill into silver town the weather began to change rapidly the extremely cold winds that howled through the silver trees the ground began to freeze around my feet and I was frozen solid and could not move. I must have fallen asleep as when I awoke I found myself in a small cottage with the windows and doors frozen shut. I remember looking thought the windows frames covered in icicles and seeing the sun shining and a beautiful summer lane full of lush green grass and flowers it was almost bizarre. As it seem so hot and sunny outside yet the small cottage was freezing cold and very damp."

"That sounds very much like a small cottage I saw near rainbow falls and when I came back passed with El'f bez imeni to show her the cottage the closer we got the further away the cottage was. It was most bizarre."

"That's as strange as at one point it felt as if the cottage was moving up hill."

"If I had known that you were probably in that cottage. I would have tried to get you out.

"That's so sweet so Alana but I think it was the work of older silver elf and she was not going to let and you or El'f bez imeni rescue me".

"Yes your problaley right" said Alana as elder grandma elf then offered Alana another piece of bread.

"Would you like another piece of walnut and ginger bread or would you like to try the apple and lime bread." As Alana tuck a slice of the apple lime.

"This bread is so yummy" she said after taking a large bite just. Just then a young Elf stopped at the table where Alana was sat.

"Would you like a hot drink" he asked.

"Yes please" said Alana as the young Elf passed Alana a hot red drink and placed a large bowl of marshmallows on the table.

"This looks and smells so amazing" said Alana

"What flavour is it"? She asked.

"It is cranberry and cherry and the marshmallows are hot honey and cinnamon with a chestnut and caramel filling"

"Thank you" said Alana as Alana began to sip the hot juice as she saw Capsuna walking towards the stone table. Capsuna then came over and sat down next to Alana.

"How's the juice" she asked.

"It is so wonderful" said a Alana with a giggle.

"So glad you like it and I still cannot believe how long it has been since I last saw you. She said as Alana and her elves friends sat chatting into the early hours just enjoying each other's company and chatting about old times.

Then all of a sudden Alana woke up in her bed and looking at the clock.

"Its only 3am. This is no time to be waking up. I need a drink." As she gets out of bed goes down stairs and into the kitchen. As Alana takes a cup out of the cupboard opens the fridge and pours herself a drink of milk. Taking the milk back upstairs with her.

"I hope I can get back to sleep quickly" she said to herself as she yawned and got back into bed. Alana then places the cup of milk on her bedside cabinet. Within seconds Alana is fast asleep back in the place where she had just been talking with Capsuna and elder grandma elf less than 5 minutes before. Alana looked around she notices that there is no one around.

The area had been deserted and much colder than it was previously. The fog becoming thicker than it been the pots left stacked on the table and the big wooden cauldron covered in cobwebs.

"I wonder where everyone is" she thought as it looks like no one has been here for some time. Then she looks over to where the soup was given out and sees a figure sat by the side of one of the trees. As Alana walks over she soon realises that it was the same Elf that served the hot drinks and marshmallows.

"Hello said Alana where did everyone go"?

"What do you mean"? Asked the Elf.

"I was sat over there with Capsuna and elder grandma elf this evening" pointing to the stone table. She said looking confused.

"That was months ago" said the Elf.

"How can that be"? Asked Alana.

"After taking to Capsuna and elder grandma elf you wondered off into the dark forest. We all waited for you to return but you did not come back I said I would wait here for you to come back".

"You waited here for me" she said.

"You're so sweet by the way what is your name"? Asked Alana.

"My name is keskiyön unelma.

"What a sweet name and it's is so lovely to see you again"

"Lovely to see you again to".

"So where did everybody go"? She asked.

"Some were captured by the darkness some managed to escape and run away deep into the forest to hide."

"Well what you waiting for lets go and find them" as she grabs hold of keskiyön unelma's hand pulling him up from the ground. As she is eager to set off in a hurry.

"Hold on what's the rush"? He asked.

"I want to find them now" said Alana.

"Well before we go rushing off we need to make a plan as to where we are going and how to rescue the other Elves."

"Ok" said Alana.

"Well ok" said Alana.

"Let's make a plan" as they both walked over to the stone table and sat down.

"So where do we go from here"? Asked Alana.

"Well first we need to grab that lit lamp of the tree so we can see our way through the forest." As Alana began to climb the tree to get the lamp and still listening to what keskiyön unelma had to say.

"I just wish this fog would lift a little bit. So we could see clearer as to know which way to go. But not to worry if we take it slow we will find our way through the dense fog and hopefully once we retch the other side of the forest the fog may have disappeared."

"Let's hope so" said Alana passing keskiyön unelma the lamp.

"Ok let's get going said keskiyön unelma; as he stood up and pulling out a large blue maple leaf from his pocket as he slowly unwrapped It. as he said to Alana.

"Would you like a piece of toffee?"

"Yes please" she said

"What flavour is it"?

"Orange and spicy chocolate toffee"

"That sounds so nice" as she takes a piece and then takes a small bite.

"Yum yum that's delicious" she says as she starts to chew the toffee. A few minutes later after finishing her toffee. Alana spots a fortune teller wearing the most wonderful poncho made from autumn leafs selling hot drinks.

"Hello my dear would you like something hot to drink"?

"Yes please" said Alana.

"But I don't have any money" she says sadly.

"You don't need money" said the old fortune teller.

"I take bags of magic in exchange for my hot drinks."

"But I don't have any bags of magic to give you either. I am really sorry. I would have loved one of your hot drinks they smell so wonderful".

"That's such a shame" said the fortune teller. After a few minutes of silence the old woman then said to Alana.

"I tell you what I can give you a small one for free."

"Aww thank you very much" said Alana.

"Which flavour would you like"? Asked the fortune teller. As she pointed to the list of drinks written on the board by the side of her cart.

"Wow they all sound so nice." Hot caramel chocolate with orange flavoured whipped cream and hot strawberry flovered with walnut sprinkles or cinnamon and nutmeg ice cream hot vanilla and chocolate fudge with lime flovered whipped cream honey roasted marshmallow ice cream with hot black cherry sauce As Alana stood licking her lips debating which drink to have.

"I wish I could try them all.

"I think I would like hot caramel chocolate with honey roasted marshmallow ice cream and black cherry sauce."

"Good" said the fortune teller as she makes up the drink and passes it to Alana.

"Thank you" says Alana with a big beaming smile on her face. Alana then takes a sip of the drink.

"Wow this is so wonderful and so tasty" just as her eyes start to close as she falls to the ground and suddenly wakes up in her own world feeling really thirsty.

She begins to sit up sliding herself to the bottom of the bed. Rubbing her eyes as she sits on the bottom of the bed slipping her feet into her slippers as she stretchers her arms as she yawns. Alana slowly stands up and walks across the bedroom and opens her bedroom door then tuning right and down the stairs and straight into the bathroom. A few seconds later she hears her grandma shout.

"Good morning Alana did you sleep ok?"

"Yes thank you grandma" she shouts back from the bathroom.

"Are you ready for some breakfast"?

"Yes please" as she opens the bathroom door walks across the hallway and enters the kitchen.

As she stands at the kitchen door her grandma standing with her back to Alana as she is cooking breakfast.

"What would you like"? Shouts grandma as she turns and notices Alana in the door way.

"Sorry I did not know you were stood there"?

"It's ok grandma" she says.

"I would like egg bacon and sausage fried bread sandwich please.

"Okay then" says grandma.

"It will be ready soon would you like any cereal why you are waiting"? She asks.

"No thanks but I would really love a milkshake do we have any black cherry ice cream left"?

"If we do it will be in the big freezer in the coal shed."

"I will go and have a look when I have made breakfast" said grandma.

"It's ok I can go and look" as Alana walks over to the back door and down the passage way and though a door at the bottom.

"Did you find any"? Her grandma shouts a few minutes later.

"Yes I found some right down at the bottom of the freezer" as she walks back into the kitchen.

"Where's the blender"? Asks Alana.

"In the cupboard at the bottom right hand corner" states her grandma. Alana then reaches down to the cupboard to get the blender and places it on the worktop. She then places her black cherry ice cream in the blender and pours in the milk as she switches on the blender full speed within a few seconds she has finished. As she switches off the blender and pours the thick and creamy ice cream milkshake into a large glass. Alana then tastes the drink.

"That's really so yummy would you like a taste grandma"?

"Yes please I would love a taste" as Alana passes grandma the glass and she takes a sip.

"That's so lovely and creamy" as grandma passes the glass back to Alana.

"Would you like me to pour you some in a glass say Alana.

"No thank you that sip was just enough for me" she says as she places Alana's breakfast on the table.

"Come on then let's sit and eat" she says and you can tell me all about your latest dreams as they sat and happily chatted as they eat.

Alana tells her grandma all about the fortune teller and how she meets keskiyön unelma.

"That sounds lovely dear and keskiyon unelma seems like such a very nice boy. I think you need to watch out for that fortune teller" says grandma as she sits sipping her cup of tea.

"Ha ha your funny grandma he is an elf not a boy.

"But all the same he seems very nice."

"Yer he is and why do you think I need to keep my eye on this fortune teller?"

"Because I think, she is up to something."

"Really".

"Yes really I do you will have to keep me up dated on your dreams and if you meet her again" says grandma as she gets up and starts to clear the table.

"As I love hearing about all your dream adventures"

"Thank you" said Alana as she gets up and gives her grandma a big hug.

"Come on then" hugging Alana back. "You need to go and get your bag packed as your mum will be here soon to collect you.

"As your back at school tomorrow"

"Ok grandma" as she leaves the kitchen and heads to her bedroom to collect her belongings.

"Are you nearly ready as your mother has just pulled up outside" grandma shouts.

"I am coming now" as Alana comes running down stairs and out the front door.

"Hang on a minute have you forgot something? " as Alana stops suddenly and turns around and runs back up to her grandma and gives her a big kiss and hug.

"That's better" says her grandma.

"You better go your mother is waiting."

Alana then turns around and runs back down the path and though the gate as she gets into the car and winds down the window.

"Bye grandma see you soon" as Alana and her mother wave goodbye to grandma standing in the doorway.

"Bye Alana" shouts her grandma waving back.

"See you again soon love you" as grandma blows her a kiss.

As Alana's mum starts to drive away Alana and her mum began to chat.

"Did you have a nice time?" Her mum asks.

"Of course I always have a good time."

"Did you go anywhere nice"?

"We went up the peak district to visit grandma's cousin Sybil and Sybil brought us lunch at the travelling gypsy"

"Is that the pub across the road from where Sybil lives?" her mum asked.

"Yes it is."

"Any way how is Sybil? Have not seen her in ages." said her mum.

"She is good we should have a ride up there sometime me, you and grandma I am sure she see would love to see you again."

"That would be nice" as her mum pulled into the drive way as Alana got out the car and headed for the front door as her mum followed behind.

"You need to go and get all your stuff ready for school while I get supper ready" said her mum.

"Why what's for supper asked Alana.

"Roast chicken"

"I love roast chicken" she said licking her lips.

"So of you go and get your school bag ready for morning and I will shout you when supper is ready but straight after supper it bath and hair wash and an early night"

"Ok then" said Alana as went up to her bedroom.

That evening after enjoying her roast chicken supper and after having had a nice soak in the bath Alana feels tried, she puts on her nightdress and gets straight into bed. Within minutes, she fell fast asleep.

CHAPTER SEVEN

As the summer turns to autumn its Alana's first day back at school after the summer holidays and in her last year of school. As she leaves her house on a cold and foggy September morning wrapped up warm with a black winter coat and a thick black scarf.

Alana closes the front door behind her. As she walks from home and down the lane. Alana soon reaches the bottom and turns the corner. Alana looks up and sees her friends excitedly waiting for her. As Alana runs over to her friends hugging each other in turn. It is the first time the four at been together since the summer break up from school. As they stood and talked for a few minutes before setting of up the road to school. The four of them walk slowly chatting away as they each in turn tell each other what fun they had going on there holidays as they head towards the traffic lights.

Having soon arrived at the traffic lights they crossed quickly, across the path and into the park walking under the trees where the autum leaves had fallen the golden leaves crunching under their feet as they walked though them as they gathered up the leaves with their hands throwing them high in the sky as they jumped up to catch them before they were carried away in the breeze.

After Alana and her friends had finished playing in the leaves they carried on their way to school still chatting away after a few minutes they came to some swings.

"Come on" said Alana to her friends looking at her watch.

"We still have half an hour till we need to be at school" as she runs over to the swings.

"Ok" her friends shout as they come running over. Dropping their school bags by the side of the swings as they giggled to each other as they began to swing higher and higher at first they could see right across the park then the fog began to become thicker and could no longer see much insight.

"Come on lets go" said Alana getting of the swing and grabbing her bag as the other girls followed.

For a moment they all stood by the swings wondering which way to go. The fog was excessively thick and far too dense to see as they stood debating which way they should go.

"The river is somewhere over there" pointing to the right.

"Lets walk slowly this way"?

"I think the bridge is over here"? Pointing straight ahead.

"Ok let's hope so" as they all linked arms as they walked close to each other. They could just about see the edge of the bridge though the fog and soon skipped across the bridge and though the foggy park up the hill and though the woods at the back of the school. Soon walking though the school gates. Just as the bell rang.

"That was good timing" said Alana

"It was indeed" said her friends as they joined the back of the line to go in for registration.

As soon as they all sat down at their desks which was four chairs around a table? Alana sat down with her three friends as the teacher read out each name in turn.

"Well that makes a change your all here" said the teacher as he closed the register and sat on the edge of his desk.

"Did you all have a nice summer holiday" he asked the class.

"Yes we did them all" said.

"What about you sir"? Asked one of the boys who was sat at the next table.

"I did thank you."

"Ok then who wants to start and tell us about their summer holiday" as Alana was now an oblivious to the conversation around her as she sat and drifted off into her own little world. Day dreaming about her adventure in her dream world as she remembered returning to the area in the woods. Where the fortune teller was serving hot drinks and the elf boy was but neither were there when she returned as she found the lamp hanging on the tree she remembered searching the woodland for them with the lamp. Walking though the crunchy crisp leaves like she had done on the way to school with her friends that morning.

"Are you with us?" the teacher asked.

Alana looked miles away day dreaming it took Alana a few minutes to register.

"Yes sir" she answered.

"Well ok then" said the teacher.

"Now then said the teacher I would like to know what job you would like to do when you leave school. I will start with"? As he looked around the class room.

"You Alana" as he pointed in Alana's direction.

"So what would you like to be when you leave school"? As Alana thought for a minute. She answered.

"I think I want to be a traveller" she said.

"That's just ridiculous" said the teacher.

"You need a job to make a living and to support yourself and being a traveller is not going to make you a living."

"Next" he said to Alana's friend Sarah who was sat next to Alana.

"I do hope the job you want to do when you leave school is a bit more sensible than Alana's choice" he said.

"Of course it is" said Sarah.

"Come on then tell the class what job you want to do when you leave school."

"I want to be a bed tester" said Sarah

"Really that's sillier than Alana's idea as Alana and Sarah sat giggling.

"It's not funny" said the teacher.

"I suppose you two could join forces and become travelling bed testers." This made Alana and Sarah giggle twice as much

"If you two Carrie on like this you will never achieve anything.

"This is your last year at school. So you should be looking to go to college or joining a job training program to further your education. The teacher told Alana and Sarah.

"With a career choice like yours you both would be better of finding yourself a young man and getting married. Because there is not much hope of you both having great careers. Just then the bell for lunch time rang.
As everybody rushed out of the classroom. Alana chatting with her friends as they arranged to meet after school. Alana was still per occupied with her dream from last night and spent the rest of her day dreaming. After school she meets with friends as they walked home from school arriving at the bottom of the lane. The friends said their goodbyes and parted ways. Arranging to meet for school again in the morning. As rushed home.
As Alana arrived home hanging up her hat scarf and coat she switched on the television in the lounge as she lay down on the sofa to watch her programs. She was asleep within in seconds and not waking up for several hours.

CHAPTER EIGHT

That night Alana was so tried from her Saturday job, that she only eats half of supper. This was fish and chip, from the local takeaway. That was one of her favourite meal so by half pass eight Alana was washed, in her nightdress and ready for bed. As she made her way up the stairs taking with her a half drank mint flavoured hot chocolate and marshmallows.
Lying in bed wondering if she should read for a little while, but she did not get the chance within seconds she had fallen fast asleep.

Within minutes, Alana was back into her dream world where she found herself back in the paddock remembering where she would often take Flash Thunder and Zero. Where Alana would spend hours with her beloved horses as she started waking over towards where the gate once was it had broken off its hinges and was rioting on the ground. The brambles and thorns had become over grown and were trailing across the floor. It was no longer the picturesque meadow it once was when Alana first came here.

Her palace it was hardly visible completely covered in ivy and thick thorns. Trees were growing though the roof as they twisted around the doors and windows. The palace had become a dark grim and eerie place. She could hear the wind whistling though the broken windows and now a deserted palace.

"I really miss how it use to be" she thought as she looked around at what was once her perfect dream. With tears in her eyes.

"Everything is changing so much and so quickly" she said as she looked up and saw the huge black clouds moving in right above where she was standing.
Just then, she felt something wet land on her shoulder.

"Is that a drop of rain I felt" she wondered. As she stretched out her hands as she felt the rain drops landed on her hands and face. She then turned around and ran bear footed towards the trees where she had found a bridge many years back. Where the pink lilies once grew, the rain began to pour and only dressed in her ankle length silk nightdress she felt the cold wind as it whipped though her whole body. Alana began to shiver her teeth began to chatter.

"I am freezing," she said as she reached the trees to shelter from the rain.

Alana then looked down at her nightdress.

"Look at the state I am in. I am filthy" as the mud and water had splashed up against the bottom of her nightdress as she ran across from the meadow to under the trees. She tried to ring out some of the water from the bottom of the nightdress. As she stood still under the trees dripping wet from head to toe. She felt the ground shake as it throws her a few meters away from where she was stood. Then she lands on her hands and knees with the water rising fast around her. Alana began to try and slowly stand as the water was moving fast. She then noticed a red bracelet in the water and bent down to pick it up. As she got a closer look Alana released that it was in fact a red gold ankle bracelet. With the words inscribed was El'f bez imeni strawberry lagoon. It is El'f bez imenis bracelet she said excitedly wonder where she is she thought looking around. Hang on a minute she though.

"Oh dear this does not really seem good" As her excitement turned to sadness as she stood looking at the bracelet. El'f bez imeni would never go anywhere without her bracelet let alone takes it off as she felt a shiver down her spine.

The water was still rising around her as she slid the red bracelet on to her arm.

"I need to find her but where do I start"? As she looked across to the once beautiful meadow.

"I think I will walk across the meadow have to start somewhere". As she waded across the water which was now waist high. It was slow going though the water but Alana knows that she had to walk though the water to get to the meadow. After sometime, Alana reached the meadow a place that was once full of life. She closed her eyes and remembered the fun she had with Flash, Thunder, and Zero the sweet smell of all the prettiest flowers that grew there the busy buzzing bees the brightly coloured butterflies and the neatly trimmed hedgerows. Now a just a cold dark burnt out wasteland smouldering under the dark cold foggy atmosphere. A land she once recognized for its beauty had now become a very different world.

A world that was becoming less familiar to her as she walked across the meadow. Half way across the meadow, it began to become hillier as Alana carried on walking. The higher she was the water became more shallow.

Then as what had seemed like walking for ages as she reached a small woodland area. The rain had become more like drizzle the sky had become a little brighter. Even the sun was trying hard to shine though the broken clouds. Walking though the woodlands, she notices the odd bluebell but most were tramped down and broken as she knelt down to pick one.

Alana could see some grave stones leaning against a wall what looked old.

"Never noticed these before"? As she started to walk over to them.

"I wonder who they belong to." As she looked at the first stone.

"Oh no please no It can't be"? As she became really upset as the tears began to roll down her cheeks' as she read the name of the first grave stone El'f bez imeni the second was elder grandma elf and the third was keskiyön unelma.

"No," she gasped as she stepped backwards then ran, as fast her legs would take her. Stopping suddenly at the top of the hill. Where she could see right down the valley that ran down the meadow. The river that had spread right across the land, as she stood still and silent. She tried to wipe away the tears with the back of her hand as she felt the cold wet wind on her face. The wind whistled as it blew though her hair.

Then she realised something was not quite right not only had she not seen a sole since she got here. She had not even heard a bird tweet or sing. This place is giving me the creeps and it is just so eerie she thought. Just as she was thinking, it could not get any worse Alana felt the ground beneath her shake for the second time. The ground pushed her forward as she began to fall trying to grab anything to stop her from falling. However, there was nothing to break her fall as she splashed straight into the water at the bottom of the hill then suddenly woke up on the floor beside her bed.

"I do not half feel ruff" as she slowly pulled herself up. She noticed the time was 8.20 am as she started to panic as she threw her duvet back on her bed. As she flung open her bedroom door and rushed down stairs as quickly as she could and in to the kitchen.

"Mum can you phone the school and tell them I am going to be late"? She said in hurried voice.

"You're not going to school today I have already phoned them."

"I came to wake you up earlier.

"You were tossing and turning and the sweat was pouring of you and you don't look well."

"I think your coming down with the flu your soaking wet though you look like you have been in a rain storm" If only you she knew she thought as her mother took her temperature.

"Just have I suspected? You have a high temperature so it's back off to bed missy."

"I will bring you up a hot drink and something to eat." As Alana went back up stairs

"Just the hot drink please," she shouted,

"I am not hungry"

"Ok and make sure you get changed. That nightdress is sopping wet."

"Ok" she shouted as she went back up stairs. Changed into a clean nightdress and got back into bed as she lay in bed thinking about her dream. About 10 minutes later there was a knock on the door.

"Come in" said Alana as the door opened and her mum peered around the slightly opened door.

"How you feeling"? "

"I am ok," said Alana.

"That's good that you're feeling a little better. I have just brought you your hot drink it is honey and lemon and I rang the doctors."

"Why I am fine," she said.

"Well what did they say"? "

"Just to take some two paracetamol every four hours" as her mum placed the drink on her bedside table along with the paracetamol and starts to fluff up her pillows.

"Well I could have told you that there was no need to phone the doctors and really I am ok so please stopping fussing," said Alana.

"It's only because I care about you."

"I know that you really do" as she stretched out her arms to give her mum a big hug.

Just as her mum was about to leave the room.

"Could you please switch me radio one on."

"I am sure you can do that yourself" said her mum

"But you have already fluffed my pillows and I am comfy."

"Oh well ok" said her mum as her mum turned on the radio and left the room.
Alana then drank her honey and lemon that her mum had brought to her and took her paracetamol. She lay down listing to the songs on the radio as she slowly began to drift off into a deep sleep appearing back in the water where she had been before.

"Oh no not this place again" she thought. But this time the water was up to her neck and it was much colder and darker than before. What am I going do? ".

 "Where do I go she thought, as I am not going back up that hill to fall back down again?" and noticed the water was still rising. Then as she was looking around caught sight of the trees on the other side. The trees are not to faraway as she headed over to towards them. As she paddled through the deep water. There must be an easier and quicker way to cross this water. As she thought about it for a few minutes.

"I know I will swim across." It did not take Alana long to swim across as she approached the trees she stretched out her hand to grab hold of one of the branches as she held on tightly and pulled herself into centre of the tree.

Now what, she thought as the water became stronger as it gushed passed Alana taking nearly everything in its path. The strong water then tried pulling Alana along with it. Alana clung on with all her strength as she felt the ground shake yet again. However, was not once this time as the ground began to shake a many of times and some of the shakes became quit violent.

"I do not like this I really do not" as the rain continued to pour the wind became stronger taking everything in its path. Even Alana had a struggle to hold as the strong winds tried pulling her away from the tree blowing her up and down into the air. Alana clung on to the branches of the tree so tightly. Then she noticed something she could no longer feel the water around her as she looked down she saw that the water was disappearing into the ground. And the ground had suddenly stopped shaking. She noticed large cracks starting to appear underneath the tree she was clung to. As the water then suddenly started to disappear through them.

"Now how am going to get down from here"? She though hanging from one of the strong branches with both hands. She then looked down hang on a minute her though. I should still be able to do the moves from my gymnastics class. Alana then swung herself a couple of times before letting go. Then as she let go and tucked her knees into her tummy placed her hands on her knees. She then summer salted through the air and landed on her feet on the other side of the cracks. Alana looked behind the cracks began to creep closer to where she had landed not knowing which way to go. She then just ran as fast as she could straight ahead towards the meadow. Once at the meadow Alana carried on running clear across the once lush green landscape until she reaches the top of the hill.

 Once at the top of the hill she rests her hands on her hips while she catches her breath as she turns around she looks down at the once beautiful valley.

"Oh I just wish it was the way it was before, everything was just so nice and easy" as she tries so hard not to get upset.
Just then she saw something move in the charcoaled blackberry bushes. Where the gate once stood at the front of the meadow.

"Wonder what that is"? As she slowly walked over stopping every so often. As she did not know what it was moving about? Many things went though her mind. As she hid behind the charcoaled blackberry bushes as she peered around the corner.

"ZERO" she shouts excitedly has he comes bounding over wagging his tail.

"I have missed you so much" As she greets him with open arms as he jumps up and licks her face.

"I am so happy to see you"? She says to Zero hugging him tightly. "You really have grown" she says. Just as he wiggles out from her arms and starts to tug on the bottom of her nightdress.

"What's wrong" she asks as he runs over to where Alana found him and back again each time tugging at her night dress.

"You want me to follow you"? As Zero starts barking.

"I will take that as a yes" as she begins to follow him as zero sits hollowing

"What's the matter"? She says as she bends down to stroke him then at that moment she notices a body lying at the side of Zero. As Alana gets a closer look. She sees the body trying to move.

"Oh no" she gasps as she covers her face with her hands. Just as she peeks though her fingers as she bends down. Hoping she can be of some help as she turns the body which is face down on to its side. As Zero desperately try's to help as Alana turns the body on to the side she is so shocked to see that it is El'f bez imeni and in such a poorly state.

"El'f bez imeni it is I Alana".

"Alana is that really you"? As she whispers trying really hard to speak.

"Yes it is" as Alana holds her in her arms as Alana then gently try's to move her in to which was once the meadow.

Once Alana had moved El'f bez imeni. She lays her flat on the ground. Again El'f bez imeni tries to speak.

"Please Alana can you help me"?

"Yes anything for you my dear what would you like me to do"? Asked Alana.

"Please could you help me find my red golden ankle bracelet"? She said so slowly.

"I don't need to find your red golden ankle bracelet"

"Why don't you need to?" asked El'f bez imeni.

"As I already have it here" said Alana as Alana takes of the bracelet from her wrist and shows it to El'f bez imeni.

"Thank you so much now here's what I need you to do for me is to hold the bracelet in the palm of your hand then put your other hand tightly on top twist one hand one way and the other hand the other way making sure the bracelet is touching both palms" she tells Alana. Slowly and having to keep stopping. As Alana then does exactly what she is asked do as Alana begins to twist the bracelet. She suddenly hears it crack.

"Oh no".

"What is it"? Says El'f bez imeni.

"I think I may have broken it"? She says sadly.

"No you have not" says El'f bez imeni.

"Lift of your top hand"

"Ok" says Alana still sure that she has broken it.

"Now lift of the top part of the bracelet." Again Alana did as she was asked as she slowly removed the top part of the bracelet a bright green light shot up high into the sky from the bracelet in the palm of Alana's hand.

"Wow" said Alana.

"That is so beautiful" as she watched the green starlit light. Light up the sky just then the green starlit light began to spread across the land transforming the landscape into the lush green land as it was once before and restoring the health and beauty of the Elf.
Alana knew and adored as Alana passed the bracelet back to El'f bez imeni as she gave Alana the biggest hug.

"Thank you for saving me" she said.

"I would save you anytime it was my honour" said Alana.

"If there is anything you ever need don't hesitate to ask"

"But I don't need anything I have everything I need right here next to me" as El'f bez imeni hugs her again. "Come on let's sit and watch the elven lights before they disappear."

"Ok" says Alana as they both sit on the grass looking up at the sky.

"The sky looks so beautiful" said Alana as she watched the green light as it shone through the clouds as the stars gleamed though.

"You should make a wish" said El'f bez imeni as they watched the green light and till it disappeared as specks of shinny green Elven dust landed on the rich green meadow as it glowed in the sunlight. Just then Alana heard something.

"What was that noise"? She asked El'f bez imeni.

"Sounded like thunder" she said.

"Oh no it is not going to rain again is it"?

"I would not have though so." Then Alana noticed a flash and something black on the Horizon quickly moving towards them.

"I don't like the looks of this" she said hiding behind El'f bez imeni as she looked over her shoulder as the sound of thunder got louder. Then she saw her two beloved horses coming towards her at Flash speed. "Well at least they live up to their names" said El'f bez imeni.

"Indeed" said Alana.

"That is one thing they do is live up to their names" she chucked. As they came racing over to Alana.

"I have missed you so much" running to greet them as she began to hug them so tightly stroking their faces as they nudged her with their noses letting her know how much they had missed her too.

"Shall we go for a ride" she asks the horses as they both nigh and bows their heads down as to say yes as like old times. Alana and El'f bez imeni then climb on the beloved horses as they ride cross the meadow and to the top of hill.

"Hey El'f bez imeni I would like to show you something I found as that rode closer to the woodland where the bluebells grow" as the climbed down from the horses.

"So what do you want to show me asked El'f bez imeni"?

"It's just under the trees" as Alana pointed out the graves stones.

"Over there" said Alana.

There are three graves stones and one has your name on it"

"I don't see the one with my name on it"? Said El'f bez imeni.

"I can a sure there was one with your name on it".

"I believe you" said El'f bez imeni.

"But there is only now two" as El'f bez imeni read the names from the stone were elder grandma elf and kesyion umlea.

"I glad you have brought me here to see the graves. But don't worry as I am pretty sure its silver magic trickery."

"So is this the work of silver elf again"? Said Alana

"I am pretty sure it is" said El'f bez imeni then Alana noticed something unusual with the bluebells

"Hey look at that bluebell it is bright red" said Alana.

"That is so unusual" said El'f bez imeni.

"As they are unique to strawberry lagoon and are not found anywhere else.

"Well there found here now" said Alana. "No there's something not right here" she said.

"But not sure what but I will find out" she said jumping back on the Flash as she turned his reins to go back down the hill.

"Come Alana" she shouted as the horse galloped towards the hill.

"Why where we going"? Shouted Alana as she claimed back on thunder as she began to follow El'f bez imeni towards the hill.

"I know just the place" she said.

"Today in strawberry lagoon the Elves hold a festival called the strawberry sunset circus."

"What's the strawberry sunset circus"? "Asked Alana.

"A beautiful festival when one day a year and the sunset lasts all day the sunset is a strawberry colour it happens on the same day once a year and it is a very special event for us Elves". There are stalls of all kinds some full of food and drinks there are fortune-teller's storytellers and magic shows and so much more, it is my favourite day of the year."

"I also know that everyone will be there as they come from far and wide"

"It sounds so wonderful." Just then they stopped at the entrance to the woodlands.

"Here will do nicely as its quiet and there's is no one around as she looked around" as El'f bez imeni tuck off her bracelet and held it in her hands as Alana had done and released a small puff of green magic.

"Hold my hand" said El'f bez imeni as it transported them instantly to strawberry lagoon once back in strawberry lagoon and on the edge of the red forest.

"Which way now"? Asked Alana looking up at the magical strawberry sunset as they rode across the red grass.

"Just over there" as El'f bez imeni pointed at a large red and black marquee pointing out though the tops of the trees on the hillside.

"Not far now" as the rode though the red forest till they came to a big open space deep inside the red forest under the strawberry sunset. El'f bez imeni and Alana could see wooden fencing set back in the trees and mountains at the back of the open space with two huge black solid iron gates. As they rode across to them.

"Here we are" said El'f bez imeni as she climbed down from Flash. Alana waited still sat on Thunders back as El'f bez imeni knocked on the huge black Iron gates.

"We will have to leave the horses here they will be fine" as Alana climbs down from Thunder as the iron gates slowly opened. Just then an Elevn-gnome appeared wearing a white strawberry print shirt with tails black trousers and a black top hat and had taken hold of the horse's reins.

"What are you doing" shouted Alana as Alana tried to grab hold of the horses reins.

"I am just taking the horses to field over there" as he nodded in the direction of the field at the side of the wooden fence.

"Don't worry they will be safe there".

"Oh ok I am sorry I did not know you worked here" she said

It's ok said the Elevn-gnome no harm done well go on then go enjoy yourself" said the Elevn-gnome.

"Oh just wait a minute" shouted the Elven-gnome as he ran back over to Alana. Still holding the horse's reins.

"I have forgotten to give you this" handing Alana a strawberry shaped bracelet.

"What's this"? Asked Alana.

"It is yours to wear till you come and collect the horses"

"Come on then Alana" shouted El'f bez imeni.

"Exactly what has taken you"?

"Oh just this" as she was shows El'f bez imeni the bracelet.

"So when I fetch the horses later. I will give it back."

"Nice" said El'f bez imeni as they both walked though the solid iron gates. Under the arch way of red maple trees hanging over the path and over the fence.
As they stood on the red grass ring there black iron fencing all the way around. Between the black iron fencing and the wooden fencing there were cafes and restaurants.
On the upper ring with outside tables and chairs with black and red umbrellas.
On the far side was several waterfalls some were black some were red with black and red roses and black and red ivy growing around them. As they both walked down the red grass steps with black iron hand rails at each side.
There was a gathering of travellers each trying to sell Alana and El'f bez imeni all sorts of weird and wonderful things. As Alana stood on the bottom step her eyes glimmered with excitement seeing all the travellers with their fancy items all talking at once all trying to sell their shinny treasures to Alana.

"This necklace is magical" said one.

"As it will transport you anywhere you want to go when wearing it."

"I have this green bracelet" said the other traveller waving it in front of Alana.

"When wearing it you will be able to get anyone you want to fall in love with you."

"I have this snow globe" said one traveller.

"How's that special" said Alana.

"Please don't say that it predicts when it is going to snow as I know that it doesn't."

"No it does not predict the weather or when it is going to snow." laughed the traveller.

"But it is a magical snow globe"

"How is a snow globe magical"?

"When you shake it and as the snow starts to settle it will show you your one true love but the magic only lasts for one go then it just becomes an ordinary snow globe ornament"

"Interesting" said Alana as El'f bez imeni grabs her by the arm.

"Come on" then shouts El'f bez imeni as she drags her away.

"What's the rush asks"? Alana.

"It's about to start".

"What is about to start"? Asked Alana.

"The show".

"What show"?

"The magical mice show" said El'f bez imeni.

"The magical what show"? She said as she looked behind her as she was still pre occupied with the travellers at the bottom of the steps trying to sell their magical goods to anyone around.

"It's the magical mice show now come on" as they ran over to a red hexagon tent with a black and red striped thatched roof. When they arrived at the door they walked up to the ticket booth.

"Two to see the magical mice show please" said El'f bez imeni handing the Elven-gnome two small bags of green magic in exchange for two tickets.

"Here you are" said the Elven-gnome as he passed El'f bez imeni the two tickets.

"Thank you" she said.

"Thank you" said Elven-gnome.

"Enjoy"

"We will" said El'f bez imeni as they both walked inside. To watch the magical mice show.

"Come on let's go and sit over there" she said pointing to some big bean bag chairs on the other side of the tent. As they sat down and made them comfy. Just then an Elven-gnome came over to where they where sat with a tray.

"Hello" he said would you like something to eat or drink"?

"I have some strawberry and red lime cheese cake and to drink I have strawberry chocolate flavoured hot chocolate topped with melted fudge with a dollop of extra thick cream he said.

"How much is it"? Said Alana.

"Oh food and drinks are included in the price of the tickets and you can have as much as you like" said the Elven-gnome.

"Then can I have some cheese cake please it sounds delightful" said Alana.

"Would you also like a drink" asked the Elven-gnome.

"Yes please" said Alana as he handed her the biggest piece of cheese cake she had ever seen as her eyes widened a big grin appeared on her face as she licked her lips as she took a big bite.

"And for you he" asked El'f bez imeni.

"Same please"

"Excellent choice" he said as he passed the drinks and a piece of cheese cake to El'f bez imeni. Just then all the chatting suddenly stopped inside the tent. As it slowly went dark as huge fountains of red and black smoke lights lit up the stage. As they came up from the ground in front of the stage as the red and black curtains opened. As red and black smoke lights then covered the floor of the stage. Then a large mouse walked across to the centre of the stage as the mouse stood up at the microphone as he cleared his throat.

"Hello all" he said as he began to talk about the show.

"Ok let's get started" he said.

"And welcome my first guest riding a horse" as everyone clapped and cheered as Alana looked around and saw everyone looking excited.

"How's riding a horse magic" she thought to herself just then all was silent again as the mouse galloped on to the stage on horseback then Alana gasped.

"Wow that magic is so cool he is really riding a horse but there is no horse there." There were also houses with no windows and doors and when the mouse opened the front door it made Alana jump. She really did not expect that there was mice skipping with ropes that could not be seen and the very last performance saw Alana looked amazed the mouse pyramid was just so jaw dropping. Just then as the last performance left the stage everyone whistled and cheered as the tent lights came back on. As Alana and El'f bez imeni got up to leave.

"How did you enjoy the show"? Asked El'f bez imeni.

"It was so amazing I loved it" she said excitedly as they chatted about the show.

"The last performance was truly amazing" said Alana.

"How exactly did they manage to do that pyramid as there was one mouse at the top an empty gap then three mice then another empty gap then five mice at the bottom and how did the mice mange to stay there was nothing holding them up and nothing below them"?.

"It's called magic" said El'f bez imeni.

"Well I love it she said I love the magic".

"I know you do" said El'f bez imeni as she linked arms with Alana. As they left the tent and stood next to the ticket booth where next asked Alana. El'f bez imeni glanced around deciding where to take Alana next. As Alana was stood waiting next to the booth that sold tickets for the magical mouse show the Elven-gnome leaned forward and asked Alana.

"Did you enjoy the show"? He asked.

"Yes I did indeed" she said to the Elven-gnome.

"Well has luck has it I have two tickets left for the next show if you would like them"?

"Yes please" she said getting all excited as she nudged El'f bez imeni.

"Come on" she said.

"Let's go and see the magical mice show again" she said.

"No because would like to show you something else amazing" said El'f bez imeni.

"Maybe later if you still really want to see it again we can."

"Oh ok" she said sounding disappointed then El'f bez imeni noticed something on the other side under the trees.

"Come on her" said to Alana as she ran across the red grass.

"I know what I want to show you" she said as Alana ran after her as they soon reached the trees where there was a large black pot of water. El'f bez imeni looked in over the edge as a fortune teller asked El'f bez imeni.

"So you want to found out your future true love"?

"No not me" she answered.

"But Alana does" as she grab Alana pushing her forward to where the fortune teller stood.

"Tell Alana who her future true love is she wants to know if there is a blue eyed boy in her future."

"No I don't" she said.

"I know you do" said El'f bez imeni.

"But you're always on about him" she said.

"No I am not" she said as they spent about the next 10 minutes in disagreement before Alana agreed.

"Ok then but how much is it to have a vision of my future true love"? She asked the fortune teller.

"Just one bag of red magic" she said.

"Oh but I don't have any bags of magic" she said.

"But I do" said El'f bez imeni as she rooted in her pocket and pulled out a small bag of red magic.

"Will this be ok"? She asked as she handed it to the fortune teller.

"That will do nicely" she said as the fortune teller held it up to inspect the small bag of red magic.

"Now all I need now is a small bit of hair from you" she said to Alana. But before Alana could say anything El'f bez imeni had snipped off a small bit of Alana's hair from the side.

"What you doing"? Screeched Alana as she held the side of her hair in her hand as she looked at where El'f bez imeni had cut her hair.

"You have cut a massive chunk out" she screamed. As El'f bez imeni laughed.

"What you worrying about it's only a few strands and hardly noticeable" she said.

"A few stands" shouted Alana.

"It's more than a few strands."

"Oh whatever said El'f bez imeni as she passed the hair over to the fortune teller.

"At least you get to see your future true love."

"But that's not the point" said Alana.

"You have cut my hair before asking me" she said.

"Well I am sorry" said El'f bez imeni. Just as the fortune teller tide some strawberry vine around the hair and placed it in the large black pot of water and sprinkled on the bag of red magic.
Then she told Alana to learn over the edge of the black pot so she could see her future true love. Alana leaned forward with El'f bez imeni on one side and the fortune teller on the other side as she closed her eyes.

"Open your eyes" said the fortune teller.

"Otherwise you will miss your vision."

"Ok" said Alana as she slowly opened her eyes to see her vision slowly fading away and caught a small glimpse of the outline of a beautiful young man before the vision disappeared forever.

"So who his he"? Asked El'f bez imeni as she put her arm around Alana as she picked her hair from the water.

"I am not sure who he is it is not someone I know yet" said Alana.

"Hopefully one day I will meet him" she said.

"I know you will meet him somewhere in the future" said El'f bez imeni.

"How can you know for sure" asked Alana.

"Just trust me I know" as they turned around and walked away as El'f bez imeni handed Alana her hair tided with the strawberry vine.

"That's no good to me now" said Alana as she held the hair in her hand.

"Just keep hold of it because if it falls into the wrong hands someone could use it for bad against you."

"Ok" said Alana.

"Hey look who's over there" said Alana.

"Who"? As El'f bez imeni looked over to the bench carved into the tree.

"Oh my" said El'f bez imeni getting excited.

"Its keskiyön unelma" as she ran over to him.

"How are you"? She asked as she hugged him.

"We thought you were gone"

"What do you mean"? He asked.

"We found your grave" said Alana and El'f bez imeni.

"Oh ok."

"But don't worry about it is just silver magic trickery" he said.

"We thought the same" said Alana.

"Anyway it is so good to see you both."

"And it's very good to see you also."

"You want one"? He said holding out a red and black paper bag.

"What is it"? Asked Alana.

"Cookie dough balls with black cherry flavoured custard filling and covered with red chocolate."

"Yes please sounds so yummy" said Alana. As she takes one and takes a bite.

"Wow where did you get these from? They are amazing" she says with a mouth full of cookie dough.

"Over there" said keskiyon unelma pointing to a food stall near to where they were sat. Next to the area and cafes on the top level.

"Come Alana" he said.

"I will buy you some if you want"?

"That would be wonderful" said Alana. As the three of them walked across the red grass and up the red grass steps and followed along the grass ring and the black iron balcony. Till they came to a stall at the end corner as keskiyon unelma walked over to purchase the cookie dough balls for Alana.
Then while he was queued up He shouted over to El'f bez imeni.

"Would you like some as well"? He asked El'f bez imeni.

"Yes please" she said.

Keskiyon unelma then having purchased the cookie dough balls all three of the friends sat down to eat at the black iron tables. Alana leaned over the balcony wow the views from here are so amazing she said look as she turned to El'f bez imeni and keskiyon unelma even the silver mountains has beautiful red water streaming down them as it shimmered in the sunset.

El'f bez imeni and keskiyon suddenly jumped up from where they were sitting and joined Alana at the balcony where you looking said keskiyon unelma over there as she pointed straight ahead that does not look like water he said sounding worried.

"Well what is it if it's not water"? Asked Alana.

"I am not sure what it is"? Said Keskiyon unelma just then everything went dark and red sparks began to shoot up from the mountains.

"So what do you think it is"? Said El'f bez imeni.

"I think it's time to run" said Keskiyon unelma grabbing Alana and El'f bez imeni by the hand as they all ran to the exit and out though the big iron gates just as the Elven- gnomes began to quickly pack everything away. There was a large red cloud hanging over the area where the strawberry sunset circus stood. And within seconds the whole of the strawberry sunset circus was packed into several tiny leather briefcases.
As the red smoke cloud that hung over disappeared into to the leather briefcases with the strawberry sunset circus.
After the Elven-gnomes finished packing up they walked off into the dense woodland carrying the leather belief cases as they slowly started to fade away and then all of a sudden disappeared.
That was so weird said Alana just a bit said El'f bez imeni.
The area where the strawberry sunset circus was had became empty flat open space once again.
Suddenly the wind began to whistle though the trees blowing red tumble weeds across the land. As the mountains started to rumble and the ground began to shake as more and more red sparks came from the mountains landing near where Alana, El'f bez imeni and Keskiyon unelma was sat.

"Come" said Keskiyon unelma has he stood up reaching out his hand to Alana? Pulling her up from the ground.

"We need to move quickly" he said as more red sparks came from the mountains. The sparks only just missing Alana as they ran towards the dense woodland with Alana still holding on to Keskiyon unelma hand as she followed him.
Just then Alana stopped suddenly.

"What about Flash and Thunder.

"I don't see them anywhere" she said sounding sad as she looked at the strawberry shaped bracelet she held in her hands as she rubbed it with her fingers just then there was a puff of red smoke and as the red smoke cloud started to clear walking towards her was an Elvin-gnome holding the reins of her two beautiful horses. As she excited ran over to the where the Eleven-gnome and her horses were waiting.

"I had thought you had gone she" said to the horses as they rubbed their faces against Alana's.

"How did you know I would still be here"? She asked the Elevn-gnome.

"You rubbed the heart shaped bracelet I gave to you" he said.

"That's so awesome thank you" she said handing back the heart shaped bracelet to the Elven-gnome.

"Anytime and thank you" he said as he quickly faded away followed by another puff of red smoke.

"Shall we get going then"? Said, Alana.

"I don't think we will be going anywhere just yet," said Keskiyon unelma.

"Why not? "" asked Alana

"Look at the ground around you" he said

"Oh my" said Alana as she clung on to keskiyon unelma and holding on to the horses Raines

"What is that"? "Asked Alana and where is it coming from asked Alana.

"Its lava and it's coming from the
Mountains" said Keskiyon unelma as Alana looked over towards the mountains at what she thought was water running down them

"What are we going to do" asked El'f bez imeni.

"I do have a small bag of blue magic left.

"I could use to freeze the lava but I do not have enough to freeze it for long" said Keskiyon unelma

"That sounds good" said El'f bez imeni

"Let's do that then" said Alana.

"Ok you both ready"?

"I am" said Alana.

"Me too" said El'f bez imeni. Keskiyon unelma then open the bag of blue magic. He released the magic on to the lava. Almost freezing the lava on impact. Alana looked down at the lava.

"Wow the ground looks like it has been covered in bright blue crystals it is so beautiful" remarked Alana.

"Come on we need to go now before the magic dies. We don't have long the blue lava won't last long. You need to leave the horse as there is not enough magic to take the horses across said Keskiyon unelma.

"But I can't leave Flash and Thunder here" she said. Just then there was a huge bang the volcano had blown its top. The horses broke their Raines and ran away into the distance away from where the lava was flowing. The red lava moving quick towards the three friends. As Keskiyon unelma grabbed hold of Alana and El'f bez imeni as the three of them quickly run across the blue lava.Half way across the blue lava began to break up. As the friends become stranded.

"What now said El'f bez imeni"?

"I don't know I will thinking of something just give me a minute"

"I don't think we have a minute" said El'f bez imeni.

"What"? Said Keskiyon unelma as he turned to see and all he could do was watch the huge wave of lava coming towards them. Just as they were all out of options. They could not believe it when a familiar voice shouted walk across the green bridge Just then a magic green bridge appeared in front of them. Alana and her friends soon began to cross the green bridge.

"Hurry" said El'f bez imeni.

"The bridge is starting to fade."
As they began to run just making it to the other side as the green bridge suddenly disappeared.

"You ok" said the familiar voice. As the three of them look around to be greeted by Elder grandma elf and Flash and Thunder. As they ran over to where she was stood. As they hugged her.

"How did you know we were here"? Asked El'f bez imeni.

"Well it was the strangest thing. I was out picking berries when I was nearly knocked of my feet by two horses. Then I realised it was Flash and Thunder. So I caught both horses and climbed on Flash and told him to take me to you."

"You really are good horses" as she hugged Flash and Thunder. Then elder grandma elf asked Alana.

"Can I borrow Flash and Thunder? As I need to sort out this mess and I know this is the work of older silver elf and she needs to be stopped once and for all."

"Of course" said Alana. As she woke up to here her grandma gently wakening her.

"Come now Alana" she wisped.

"You to get up if you want to go to the horses today." That was the last time for many years Alana would see the strawberry elves.

CHAPTER NINE

Many years had passed Alana never really forget the about the amazing dreams she had as a child.
The dreams had become more like distant memories.
The people she had met and the places she had been in her childhood dreams sometimes wishing that she could go back and relive the beautiful dreams.

She once had as a child even if it was just for a few minutes.
But Alana now all grown up knew that she had responsibilities. She had met someone Alana thought she wanted to spend her life with.
But deep down she was not happy he was not her true love. She had hoped that new century would bring her bliss and she would find her true love but neither happened. Her relanoship fizzed out over time. Then one summers day all of a sudden. Alana was sat in her garden drinking a cup of tea when two young magpies landed by the fence.

"Good morning magpies" she said as they were searching for food.
One of the magpies looked over to where Alana was sat as one of them knocked over a dandelion. The dandelion fairies floating about as she sat and watched them. Just then one came tumbling down and landed on her lap looking down she smiled, then slowly scooped it up with her hands then lifting her hands in the air Alana blow the fairy high into the sky. As she made a wish. Then within a second she had remembered something from her childhood. She leaped up ran into the kitchen and up the stairs and into her bedroom. Looking up on the top of the wardrobe. Alana saw the little red box.

"It's in there" she said to herself getting all excited.

"Now then how am I going to reach the box" she thought looking around for something to stand on.

"I know" looking at the radiator that ran under the window and down the side of the wardrobe she then put one foot on the radiator and then pulled herself up by grabbing the corner of the wardrobe with her free hand. Alana started routeing around in the box pulling one piece out at a time.

"No that's not it nor is it that". Then finally she had found what she was looking for.

"Its here" she gasped excitedly and just at that second forgot where she was stood as she began to lose her balance. She tried to steady herself but it was no use still holding on to her piece of paper she had found in the box she fell to the ground with such a thud.

What seemed like moments later? Alana opened her eyes as she looked around as she started to feel a little bit confused.

"This is not my bedroom" she said as she tried to sit up.

"So you're a wake at last"? Said a voice as Alana looked around the room.

"What the hell am I doing here? But more to the point why am I here"? She said as she started to panic.

"You're in safe hands try not to worry".

"What do you mean try not to worry? of course I am going to worry I have just woke up in a strange place with all these wires and machines sticking in and out of me and you are telling to not worry".

"Please calm down"

"I am only a nurse"

"I am calm" said Alana.

"I just want some answers as to how I ended up here."

"Ok hang on then"

"Let me go and fetch the doctor he will be able to tell you everything you need to know" as the nurse went out of the door moments later she returned with the doctor.

"Hello Alana the doctor" said as he pulled up a chair and sat next to the bed for the next few minutes the doctor sat silent as he looked though Alana's notes as he rubbed his chin with his hand and nodded as he analyzed the charts he was looking at.

"You didn't half give us scare when the ambulance brought you in 3 days ago" he said. As he looked up at Alana.

"It's a really good job that your neighbour found you when she did. You had a fallen you had cuts and bruises you also had prolonged bleeding which we got under control but you needed a blood transfusion." said the doctor

"We have found that you do have a mild blood disorder but you can still live a normal healthy life it just means that your blood does not clot to well so a healthy diet high in iron will help and you will be fine you can go home in a few days also for a little while you will need regular checkups"

As the nurse put down the cup of tea on the table beside the bed, she asked Alana if she would like the television on,

"Yes please" said Alana

"What would you like to watch?" asked the nurse as she started to flick though the channels.

Do you have any music channels?

"Yer I think so" as she continued to go though the channels, one by one.

"Stop this one will do" said Alana.

"Ok then I will leave you for a while and I will be back soon" said the nurse as the nurse was about to leave the room she noticed a piece of paper with Alana's name on it.

"I believe this is yours" said the nurse handing Alana the piece of paper.

"You had it in your hand when you arrived and you would not let go of it."

"Thank you" said Alana as the nurse left the room.

Alana looked at the paper and smiled it is my drawing of strawberry lagoon I really miss strawberry lagoon I would love to go back there one day.

As she closed her eyes imagining what it would be like to go back to strawberry lagoon all grown up. Then she heard familiar song. A song she loved and always made her smile. As Alana opened her eyes to see the video of Dragostea Din Tei.
She noticed the beautiful boy with the cutest smile in video with the most amazing blue eyes. The type of eyes that dreams are made of.
That then made her then think about the little boy from her dreams something Alana had not done for many years. She remembered how the little boy had the most remarkable blue eyes that sparkled so brightly. I wonder if I will ever find him she sighed but the song also reminded her of her childhood dreams of wanting to travel east and her biggest dream of all travelling to Russia.

Over the next few days while still in hospital she drew up plans for what she saw was going to be the most exciting time in her life.

As from that day, she promised herself she would live the life she had always wanted to since childhood it was going to be a whole new start she was going to travel to so many new lands like in her childhood dreams Alana thought about her living her dreams to the full in the past but this time she was more determined than ever and nothing or nobody was going to get in her way within the next few days she left hospital having made a full recovery and returning home as she looked around her living room and walked over to the big mirror on the wall as she looked at herself in the mirror things are going to be very different from now she said to herself I am going to find my true love her eyes shining and with a big grin appeared on her face.

CHAPTER TEN

Only a few months left to go to her trip of her life time Alana nearly has everything in place for her trip as she just waits for her new passport and her visa to arrive. So that she can enter the Russian federation. Feeling really excited as Alana waits patiently for her documents to arrive she decides to look up and book a session to see a dream specialist as Alana sits down at her desk and types in dream specialist into her computer several come up on the page and not too far from the area she lives in. She then begins to scroll down one of them catches her eye this one sounds good as she pick up her phone and dials the number from the screen in front of her as the phone rings a few seconds later a nicely spoken lady answers.

"Hello dream to dream my name is Martha how may I help you"? Said the voice.

"Hello my name is Alana I would like to know a little bit more about your services" she asked.

"Sure" said the lady on the other end of the phone.

"Ok" said Martha.

"First of all we only do two hour sessions"

"That's fine."

"And they cost between £75-£150 if you go for the £150 one that will include three two hour sessions and a written document amazing your dreams."

"Ok the £150 sounds good so when do you have a next available session"?

"Just let me have a look in the dairy"? As the line goes quiet for a second.

"You're lucky as we have had a cancellation for tomorrow afternoon at 2pm."

"Perfect now how do I pay you"? Said Alana.

"You can pay when you come in tomorrow? If you wish and you can pay the £150 in one lump sum or two payments of £75".

"Ok that's sounds good and I will see you tomorrow bye for now" says Alana.

"Goodbye" says Martha as Alana puts down the phone and notices the time.

"Oh my it's nearly supper time" as she walks into the kitchen and opens the fridge. As she looks inside what should I have she wonders?

"I think jacket potatoes with cheese and coleslaw Alana then also sees the strawberries at the top of the fridge.

"But with what I know I will stick them in the blender mix in some chocolate" as she opens the cupboard and reaches up as she takes out a large bar of chocolate and some pitta breads as Alana washes the strawberries.

She blends the strawberries for a few seconds on high speed then picks up the bar of chocolate as she open the packet thinking how much she should need decides to put in the whole bar in.

"No point in wasting good chocolate" she chuckles to herself.

After switching on the blender full speed again Alana the takes some pittas from the packet and pours on the strawberries and chocolate. Then places them in the fridge after about half an hour.

Alana then returns to the fridge about half an hour later.

"Nicely done" she says as she presses the finger on the top of one the chocolate and strawberry pittas. Which has hardened nicely then placing the pittas on the worktop.

Alana then adds a dollop of whipped cream on the top.

That evening Alana had a relaxing evening soaking in a nice hot bath with a large mug of hot chocolate and marshmallows then slipping into her pyjamas as snuggled under her half quilt. She chilled out on the sofa as she sat and watched some television before going to bed around 11.30 pm.

The next morning as Alana woke up and looked at the clock it was early just gone 6.30 am.

"It's just too early and I was having such a lovely dream" as she tried to go back to sleep as Alana lay a wide awake for about 1 hour.

"I can't get back to sleep I may as well get up and have breakfast" she said yawning. Alana slide herself out of bed and went in to the bathroom a few minutes later she went down the stairs and into the kitchen as she got out the cornflakes and switched on the kettle. Leaning against the work top.

"Wow that was such a lovely dream I had last night I was lying down in my meadow. It was summer time with the most beautiful blue sky I had ever seen with just a few fluffy white clouds as she smiled.

"Then I got up and boarded an old fashioned stream train that travelled though some purple mountains. Which was topped with beautiful crisp white snow that gleamed in the bright sunlight as the train went around the mountains.

I remember getting off at the top and looking down on the valley below. There was no one else around and for that moment I had the whole world to myself and not a single sound. Even the waterfall down below looked frozen in time not even the slightest breeze."

As she then sat down on the ledge of the mountain dangling her feet over the edge as she started to play with her hair.

"But then I woke up to the busy noise of the outside world I just wish I could have stayed there for just a little while longer" she sighed.

"It was so very peaceful oh well" she said as she yawned again as she lifted the freshly boiled kettle to make a cuppa tea then pouring out the corn flakes in the bowl after adding milk to her cuppa of tea and cornflakes. Alana sat down at the table to eat as she read the morning newspaper.

"Not much interesting news" she said as flicked though the pages of the paper

After breakfast Alana washed the pots watered the garden pegged out the washing and had a shower as she got ready to go to her appointment. Straightens her hair and dressing herself in a red t-shirt black jacket black leggings and black heeled boots at 1-30pm. She was ready to go and telephoned a taxi locked her front door and waited outside on the front for the taxi arrive. She did not have to wait long about 5 minutes as the taxi pulled up she got in and told the driver where she was going.

"Ok" he said as that set off as they began to chat.

"Lovely weather for this time of year" he said.

"It is indeed just hope it stays like it for a while"?

"I do hope so to" as the taxi stopped.

"Is this the place"?

"Yes it is thank you."

"That will be £5.20 pence please" ok as Alana passes £6.00 to the taxi driver.

"There you are" as she passes the driver the money."

"Keep the change as she opens the door to get out.

"Thank you have a nice day see you again soon"

"Will do thank you" says the taxi driver as she closes the door.

When Alana arrives at the reception desk the receptionist is busy on the computer and talking on the phone. After a few minutes of waiting the lady hangs up the phone and comes over to Alana.

"How may I help you" she asks.

"Hi my names Alana and I have an appointment at 2pm" she says.

"Oh yes" says the lady as she looks in her dairy.

"You're a little early but that's ok."

"I wanted to get here a little early as I would like to pay the £150 for the three sessions" as Alana hands over the money.

That's fine" says the receptionist as she counts the money.

"Would you like a tea or coffee?" while you wait" she asks.

"Tea please milk no sugar"

"Ok" said the lady. As Alana takes a seat in the waiting area as she starts flicking though some magazines on the table just then the lady reappears with a cup of tea.

"Here you go there's your cup" of tea.

"Thank you" says Alana.

"Your welcome you should not have to wait much longer" she says. Just then a man appears in the doorway with a clip board opposite from where Alana is sat.

"Hello my name is Andy" he said with a smile on his face as he walked over towards Alana as Alana stood up from where she was sat as they both shook hands.

"Nice to meet you" Alana.

"Likewise" says Alana.

"Ok then shall we get started"? As they both entered the room.

"Please take a seat" said Andy as he switched on the kettle.

"Would you like another tea or coffee"?

"No thank you not at moment maybe a little later".

"Ok then let's get started".

"So Alana can you tell me about your early childhood dreams as far back as you can remember."

"I have had very vivid dreams all my life but there was always one place in particular were I would always return a place. I felt safe and happy."

"So what do remember about this place"? He said as he was writing down notes.

"I remember everything from the silver castle to the meadow where I rode my two beautiful horses with Zero the dog in the beautiful meadow. Where the buttercups grew and the birds would sing so beautifully.The lane where the sweet smelling wild flowers would grow all year long and the sun always shone."

"Sounds beautiful" said Andy.

"Then one day I had been watching the horses and Zero play in the paddock. I wondered off to pick some flowers and found a bridge I had never seen before and after that everything started too changed."

"How old were you then"? Andy asked.

"I was around 9 nearly 10 years old at the time."

"So what happened"? He asked.

"I just remember waking up and everything was red including the sky and trees I meet a lovely young elf and we have been friends like forever since then and she took me to her village called strawberry lagoon. Where I meet many other elves and a beautiful boy with the most amazing blue eyes and so sweet".

"Very fascinating" he said as he rested the clip board on his lap. As he listened intently his hands resting on top as he nodded in agreement. As Alana continued to tell Andy about her childhood dreams. How when she went though her teenage years her dreams became more erratic. Over the three sessions. Alana told Andy all of dreams and how they had made an impact on her life. As Andy analysed her dreams. Andy told her how her dreams were just another reality we must live. And how the little boy with the amazing blue eyes in her dreams was her perfect man. Her true loves in both realities Alana need to find him in this reality to feel complete.

A few days after her last dream therapy session Alana felt happy and contented.
Just then there was knocking at the door as Alana opened the door her face lit up.
It was what she had been waiting for her passport and travel documents had arrived as the courier hand them to Alana.

"Just need you to sign here" he said.

"Hope you have a wonderful time in Russia"? He said has he been leaving.

"I will thank you" she said as she closed the door.

"Yay I am going to Russia" she said exactly as she ran upstairs in her bedroom and pulled out the suitcase from under her bed and opened her wardrobe.

"What should I take with me"? she sighed as she went though each item of clothing after several hours of packing and unpacking she had packed a few dresses several pairs of jeans and trousers and several tops and t-shirts her underwear and socks her favourite strawberry shower gel. Alana tried every which way to close the suitcase as it was bursting at the seams but evenly she did manage to close the suitcase as Alana dragged it down stairs and left it by the front door.

"I just need to arrange my tickets and hotel" thought Alana. As she walked into the living room and sat down. And turned on her computer. Alana then scrolled down of all the travel options. Quickly deciding the best way to travel to Russia. Alana had made up her mind. She would travel by train to London then fly to Riga. Once in Riga Alana would then take the bus to Russia. Then having booked her train and plane tickets.

"Now then I have my train and flights booked just need to book a hotel." Alana then spent the rest of the afternoon looking for the perfect hotel.

"I have found the perfect hotel" she beamed after searching for a long while. It was a small hotel with an extra large king size bed with a personal bathroom and room service. The location was also just perfect in the heart of Moscow on the edge of red square. A popular tourist area within Moscow and some of Russia's most beautiful bars and restaurants. By now it was late afternoon.

"I must make a move if I am going to make this train on time" she said as Alana picked up the telephone to book a taxi after a few minutes a lady answered the phone.

"Local taxis how may I help you"?

"Can I book a taxi to the train station please"?

"What time would you like your taxi to arrive"? Asked the lady on the other end of the line.

"Straight away please" said Alana.

"No problem it's on its way"

"Thank you" said Alana has she hung up the phone. Just then she heard the taxi pull up outside as she grab her coat her passport and documents as she open the front door and dragging her suitcase with her. Alana then closing and locking the front door behind her and walking through the gate. Just as the taxi driver came over to help Alana to put her suitcase in the taxi. The taxi then slowly pulled away from Alana's house.

"Going anywhere nice"? Asked the taxi driver.

"Yes" I am going to Russia."

"Sounds lovely I have always wanted to go there. Have you been before?" he asked.

"No this is my first time. I had hope to go to a concert to see my favourite singer but my travel documents did not arrive in time" she said sadly just as the taxi pulled up at the train station as Alana paid the driver as he lifted out her suitcase and placed in on the pavement

"Hope you enjoy your travels."

"I will thank you and I hope you get to go to Russia someday".

"I hope so too" said the taxi driver as they both parted ways and said goodbye to each other. Alana then walked into the train station and over to the counter to pick up her tickets she had booked earlier.

"Which platform will the train arrive"? Asked Alana.

"Platform 6 you better hurry as the train will arrive in 5 minutes"

"Thank you" as Alana grabs her tickets and suitcase as she rushes over to platform 6.
Arriving at platform 6 Alana sees the train has arrived. With the wind blowing through her hair Alana boards the train. Alana then quickly finds a seat as the train pulls out from the station. Once seated Alana takes out her headphones and her favourite playlist. Closing her eyes knowing her dreams are coming true. As the train speeds towards London and still hoping that she may find her true love in Russia.

THE END

Printed in Great Britain
by Amazon